The Secret of Eden Park

By

Susan Biscoe

ISBN: 0-75964-711-9

This book is printed on acid free paper.

1stBooks - rev. 06/22/01

Prologue

"Why not?" Timmy asked timidly.

"Because we're swinging here, and we don't want you near us, okay?", Missy answered, the venom in her voice matching the hateful look on her face.

The little boy looked around, and seeing his mother a comforting distance away, made a decision.

"You can't tell me what to do," he said. "I can use that swing, if I want to. It doesn't belong to you."

As he started toward it again, Missy jumped off the one she was on, and started swinging on the one he had been headed for. Now the only swing left was the one that was between the two girls.

Seeing Timmy's slight hesitation, Missy immediately said, "I guess I can't stop you from using that swing, but I have to warn you, we're not very good at keeping these things straight, and we just might swing right into you-HARD."

Timmy's courage evaporated. With one last look at the swing, he turned around and quickly headed for the slide.

The other little girl said, "Missy, that was awfully mean. Timmy wouldn't have bothered us, why couldn't you just let him use the swing?"

"Because he's a stupid little cry baby," Missy answered. As she looked in the direction Timmy had gone, a satisfied look crossed her face. She began to swing higher and higher, laughing out loud. The other little girl, shook her head. She didn't like what Missy had done, but it was over now, and she didn't want to get into a fight over it.

As was his usual practice, he had stopped in a park to enjoy the warm Saturday afternoon. He loved the parks because of the trees. They reminded him of his own woods that had been gone for so many years. He always sat right at the edge of the woods, farthest away from anyone else. Today there were many children there, with and without parents. It amazed and pleased him, that with two missing children, some parents would still let their own go off by themselves.

When he first saw her she was on the swings with another little girl. He didn't pay much attention to her at first, because she didn't seem to be the type he was looking for. Then he noticed a little boy approach them.

There was one empty swing, and he headed toward it. The blond girl said something to him, and he stopped. He started toward it again, and she said something else. The boy stopped again, looking like he wasn't sure what to do.

This was starting to look like a situation the man was interested in, so he turned on the listening device he had purchased at the electronics store, and put the ear piece in his ear. At first it had been difficult for him to pick up the conversations he was interested in, but with practice he had been able to screen out the other noises, and concentrate only on what he had to hear. The man stared at Missy with hate in his eyes. Yes, I guess she is the kind I'm looking for, he thought. But he would have to watch her closely for a while-just to be sure.

Chapter 1

Rachel sat at her kitchen table waiting for Sara. She would be over soon for coffee, and their usual gabfest. They got together each morning to drink coffee and talk over their day to day problems. Not that they ever solved any of life's great difficulties, but at least they could air their grievances, and have someone to listen, and sympathize.

They had been friends for years, ever since they had worked together at a department store in town. They had both been married then, but neither one had children. Now, years later, Sara had two sons, Joey who was ten, and Taran who had just turned thirteen, and Rachel had nine year old Amanda, and seven year old Brian.

As Rachel waited for Sara she could hear Amanda and Brian in the next room, bickering as usual. They were playing some kind of board game, Amanda was yelling at Brian because he wasn't playing right, and Brian was complaining that she was cheating.

Rachel listened for a while, hoping they would work it out themselves.

When she couldn't take it anymore, she yelled, "All right, put the game away!"

"But Mom, I'm winning."

"Of course you're winning, Amanda, you always win" Rachel countered "but that doesn't stop you from yelling at Brian while you're winning, and I don't want to listen to it anymore."

"Well he was moving the wrong way, and he kept doing it after I told him three times. He's so stupid."

"All right that's it Amanda, I've had it with your mouth. Now put the game away, go to your room, and don't come out until you can be nice to your brother."

Amanda threw all of the game pieces into the box, and stalked off to her room, while Brian sat there watching her with tears starting to form in his eyes.

Rachel wiped his eyes, gave him a hug, and said, "Why don't you go out and play on the swings for a while. She didn't mean what she said, she's just a grouch today."

The trouble was, Rachel knew that she did mean it, and as she watched Brian go out the door, she wondered for what seemed like the millionth time why Amanda was always so mean to him.

Amanda had such a wide range to her personality that Rachel never knew what to expect. At times she could be the sweetest little girl, and at other times she could be defiant, insolent, and downright mean. It was like riding an emotional roller coaster.

Brian, on the other hand, was shy with strangers and very sensitive. He cried easily when he was hurt, but not from physical injuries. He could skin his knee, or bump his head, and he would continue playing as if nothing had happened. But when his feelings were hurt, usually by Amanda, his eyes would quickly well up with tears. Because of the difference in their personalities Rachel tended to be protective of Brian, which made Amanda feel he was spoiled, and got away with everything.

Just then Sara came in, and when she saw the look on Rachel's face, she said, "Trouble already? It's only 9:00 A.M."

"With Amanda trouble starts as soon as she's out of bed."

"Rachel! Don't talk like that."

"I know, I know, but she can't hear me, I sent her to her room. Sara, how is it that your boys seem to get along so well, and my two kids are always fighting?"

"My kids fight with each other all the time. Actually, Taran and Amanda have the same personality, which is really amplified in Taran because he is now that dreaded species-a teenager. The only difference is Joey's personality. Most things just roll off his back, while Brian takes everything to heart. Just hang in there, some day Amanda and Brian may actually be friends."

"I just hope I'm still around to see it," Rachel answered skeptically.

"So, other than World War III, how's it going?" Sara asked.

"Same as usual I guess. I wanted to get some wall to wall carpet for the living room, but Michael said it would be a waste, because we'd have to leave it here when we moved. Sara, I wish we owned our own home like you do. Michael will only do the most minimal of maintenance around here, because he considers anything else wasted money."

"Have you been looking?"

"Sort of, but with the rent so cheap here, everything we looked at within that price range is either practically condemned, or in a really seedy part of town."

"Well don't even consider anything too far away. I like you living right around the corner, and I don't know what I'd do if you moved clear across town."

"Well, don't worry about it, because it doesn't look like we'll be going anywhere for a while. It's not that I don't like this house, and I know that this rent for a five room single family is a steal, but it's not mine, you know what I mean?"

"I know, but have faith Rachel, you'll find what you want, just be patient."

"I hope so, I know it's probably not realistic, but I just have this feeling that if we find the right house everything will be perfect. But enough about me, how are Scott and Taran getting along? Any better?"

"Not really, it just frustrates me so much, because Scott really can be a good father. He takes the boys fishing, and camping, and loves doing things with them, but it's the day to day stuff that drives me crazy. He's extremely hard on Taran, always lecturing him on everything he does from leaving a light on, to not cleaning his room, to having his stereo too loud. They're constantly battling, and they always seem to put me in the middle."

"Well, don't let them."

3

"Easier said than done. Rachel, have Brian and Amanda ever failed to rope you into the middle of their arguments?"

"Point taken, maybe we both need work on that."

"Well, when you find the magic formula let me know, okay? In the meantime, I keep trying to get Scott to lighten up."

"Isn't it strange that all I really want is a home of my own, which you have..." Rachel began.

"...and all I want is a laid back, easygoing husband, which you have," Sara finished. "How do we ever manage to avoid the green eyed monster?"

"It must be our extreme level of maturity, and the fact that if we ever got to the point that we weren't speaking to each other, we'd last three days before we exploded."

"You've got that right," Sara agreed "If it weren't for these morning therapeutic bitch sessions I'd have to spend a fortune in therapy, but I guess this session will have to 'be continued'. My kids were still sleeping when I left, and I want to get back home before they wake up. Let me know how the house hunting goes. See you later."

After Sara left, Rachel thought about what they had talked about. Sara had called Michael "laid back and easy going" as if that were a *good* thing. If she only knew! That was the thing about Michael that bothered Rachel the most. He wasn't "laid back and easy going", as much as he was lazy and self centered. He always used the fact that they didn't own this house as an excuse not to do anything. He went to work at 5:30 in the morning, came home at 2:30 in the afternoon, and as far as he was concerned his day was done. He let Amanda and Brian do just about anything they wanted to do, just as long as it didn't interfere with his peace and quiet. Rachel could feel herself getting angrier, and angrier, and decided she'd better get her mind onto something else, for her own sake.

She opened the morning paper, turning to the real estate section as usual, and felt the excitement start to grow in her stomach as soon as she spotted the ad.

Rollins Avenue? A house for sale on Rollins Avenue? And within their price range? She immediately called the Realtor, and made an appointment to see the house that evening.

Unless the house was falling apart, she was sure this would be the one. EDEN PARK! This house was in Eden Park. Maybe Sara was right after all, and she *would* find what she wanted.

Chapter 2

Eden Park was the kind of neighborhood in which Rachel Palmer and Sara Spencer had dreamed of living. In fact, it was the exact neighborhood. Whenever they went through one of their frequent "let's get healthy" kicks, and would go for a walk every evening after dinner, they always walked through Eden Park. It wasn't far from where they lived, and they loved the neighborhood. Although it was not the most exclusive area of Crestwood, when Rachel and Sara would walk there, they would marvel at the beautiful homes, the well kept lawns, and envy the people that lived there. They loved walking through that area, because it was so safe.

At least that's what they thought!

Rachel and Michael looked at what was to become their dream house that very evening. The house wasn't exactly what they wanted. The living room and dining area were combined, and they would prefer to have them separate, but they could always put up a wall. The kitchen was small, and Rachel had always wanted a large country kitchen, but they could always add on later. After all, this was *Eden Park*, she was happy to make some concessions.

The owner had been transferred, and had to move very quickly, so the house was already vacant. The closing took place within a few weeks, and before Rachel knew it, she was moving into her very own home.

Sara was happy for Rachel, and spent many hours helping her to paint, pack, and move, but she couldn't help being a little envious. Since the Spencers already owned their own home, Sara figured they would just live there forever, but the more she thought about it, the more she really wished they could move. Scott wasn't really happy with the neighborhood. Their next door neighbors were loud and obnoxious, and he constantly complained about them.

Sara's sons had lived in this house all of their lives, and when they were younger, they were happy

6

there. When they started school, however, they made other friends. Joey had a lot of friends, and most of them lived in Eden Park. Because a state highway separated the two neighborhoods, they had to be driven to each other's houses when they wanted to play together.

Taran's only close friends also lived in Eden Park, and although he was old enough to walk there, it was hard for him to make plans with his friends to get together outside of school.

Then the impossible happened! They heard of another house in Eden Park that would be going up for sale.

The house seemed almost perfect for the Spencers. The neighbors were quiet, which made Scott happy. Most of Joey's friends lived in the neighborhood, and Taran's best friend lived right next door. This made the boys *very* happy. As in Rachel's case, the house itself was not exactly what Sara had dreamed of, but that didn't really matter. It was *Eden Park*. They made an offer on the house even before it officially went up for sale, and when their offer was accepted, they immediately put their home of sixteen years up for sale and looked forward to the excitement of moving.

So, two months after Rachel and her family moved to Eden Park, Sara and her family joined them. They lived two streets away from each other, and couldn't be happier. It was a beautiful, safe, upper middle class section of town.

Their children could play outside without fear. They could take their after dinner walks in their own neighborhood, and feel safe themselves. They both thought they had finally realized their dreams.

They had no idea what dark secrets this perfect neighborhood was hiding, and never imagined that their dreams would soon turn into a nightmare that they never would have believed possible.

Chapter 3

Every evening, in Eden Park, you will see many of the residents taking a healthy walk. People walking in couples, with friends, and sometimes alone. Some walked to keep in shape, others for the company, or a chance to leave the kids and dirty dishes to Dad. Rachel and Sara walked for the sheer enjoyment of checking out the neighborhood. They would notice everything from a newly painted house, to an interesting flowerbed, or a new addition. All of the homes in Eden Park were well kept, with manicured lawns and crafty lawn ornaments. All but one. The house of secrets.

It was located at the end of Rocky Ridge, the part of the road that extended beyond where Hillside ended. That part of the street, and only that part, was unpaved. The house itself was always dark at night, with heavy drapes drawn to cover all of the windows. During the day, the curtains were open, but there never appeared to be anyone at home. When the drapes were open, you could notice something peculiar about the big picture window. There was something that looked like a big metal gate completely covering the window, *on the inside*!

The only sound you heard coming from the house was the occasional howl of dogs. No one was quite sure how many dogs there were, no one had ever been close enough to count, but the sounds were enough to keep away any trespassers.

No one ever remembered meeting the resident, or residents, of 18 Rocky Ridge. If it weren't for the dogs, you might have thought that the place was deserted. Children rode their bikes past the house, and didn't give it a second look. The evening walkers strolled by, and didn't give it a second thought. Everyone had gotten so used to the house that it almost seemed normal. It might have remained that way for God knows how long if not for Rachel Palmer's "overactive" imagination, or more accurately, *intuition.*

Rachel and her family were just finishing dinner as Rachel rushed to clear her plate.

"Sara and Christie will be here soon," she told her husband, Michael, as she slipped on her walking shoes. She looked across the table at Brian as he tried to force himself to belch louder than he did the night before. Amanda groaned in disgust, while Michael just reached for what was left of the mashed potatoes.

As Rachel tried to explain to Brian what "proper table manners" meant, Amanda jumped in with, "It's no wonder you never get invited to eat at anyone's house. You're so gross."

Rachel immediately barked at Amanda to mind her business and stop being so mean, as Brian lowered his head, with tears in his eyes.

Meanwhile, Sara was also anxiously getting ready to leave her house. They were having Chinese food tonight, and Joey was pretending the lo mein noodles were really long night crawlers.

"Umm, nothing like worm guts to satisfy your hunger," he said. Taran, who never could take that kind of talk while he was eating yelled, "Cut it out you idiot, you're making me sick."

Scott, who didn't find it necessary to correct Joey's table manners, was quick to shout at Taran for calling his brother an idiot. At this point, Sara was really anxious to leave before she lost her dinner first, and temper second.

"I'm leaving for my walk," she shouted, as she headed out the door.

Christie, the youngest of the three women, managed to have her dinner dishes on the rinse cycle, and her toddler Jimmy's bath prepared before she had to leave.

Her husband, Danny, was complaining about having to give his son a bath again.

"Can't you take your walk after he's in bed?" he asked.

"Danny, you know I get really stressed walking after dark, and besides I have to deal with him all day while you go to your cushy job, and have conversations with people who actually talk in complete sentences. Rachel and Sara will be waiting for me, so I'm leaving."

The three women met in Rachel's driveway, and began their walk.

"Which way are we going tonight?" Rachel asked.

"Let's go over Hillside, down the dirt road, and around," answered Sara.

"Do we have to go down Rocky Ridge?" Christie asked, timidly.

"What's the matter?" Sara laughed. "Are you scared?"

"I just don't want to get Rachel started again," said Christie.

"Oh, like you don't think there's something strange about that house," Rachel said, defensively. "It gives you goose bumps, just to go by it."

"It's not the house that gives me goose bumps, as much as the things that go through your mind when you see it." Christie countered.

"Come on you two, you're starting to sound like my kids" Sara quipped.

The three of them began to laugh, and started on their way.

"By the way, Christie, we are going down Rocky Ridge," Sara said. "You know we have to hit all of the streets in Eden Park, or we won't get our full 3 miles."

"Can't we just go down Hillside twice?" Christie asked, and the three women laughed again.

Eden Park actually consisted of only six streets. Hillside, Christie's street, and Sunrise are off of the state highway. Rollins, Rachel's street, is off of Hillside. Rocky Ridge is parallel to Rollins, and extends past Hillside, down to Sunrise. Heritage, where Sara lives, is parallel to Rocky Ridge. Bronson starts where Sunrise ends, and circles all the way around to Rollins.

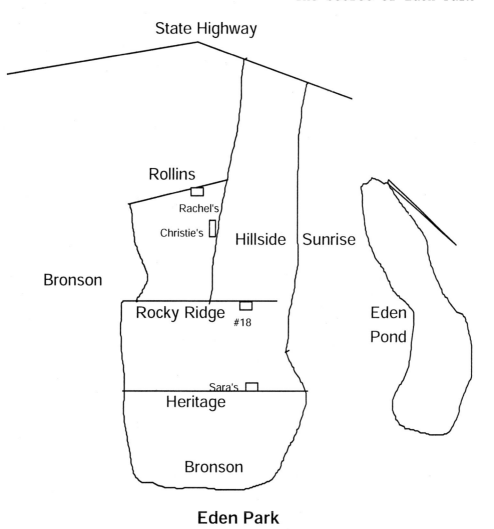

Eden Park

As the three women began their walk, they headed down Hillside, and then turned down the dirt road.

"Why do you think they never paved this part of Rocky Ridge?" Rachel wondered.

"Probably because there's only one house on this part of it," answered Sara. "Besides, don't you think it kind of fits the surroundings?"

"I know what you mean," said Christie. "That house, all by itself on a dirt road, just looks sort of natural."

"There's nothing *natural* about that house," Rachel said.

"There you go again!" cried Christie. "I knew if we went this way your imagination would start acting up again."

Rachel stared at the house, and became quiet, lost in her own thoughts. As it happened the house at 18 Rocky Ridge is directly behind Sara's house. Rachel had asked Sara if she could see anything of the house from her back yard, but since there were several storage sheds lined up across the back of the property, there was nothing to see.

This house, and it's unseen occupant, or occupants, had been on Rachel's mind almost constantly for weeks. She had joked about it with Sara and Christie, but it was not a joke to her. She really felt there was something wrong about it, but didn't know what to do.

She thought that if Sara and Christie knew she was serious, Sara would think she was crazy, and Christie would lock herself in her house forever. But, she knew she couldn't go on like this much longer, or she *would* go crazy. She was going to have to take a chance that her friends would trust her intuition, and help her figure out what to do about it. She wasn't sure yet how she was going to bring it up, but she knew it had to be soon. Something was going on inside of that house, she felt it. She also felt that the longer she waited, to find out what it was, the worse it would be.

Chapter 4

There they were again. Those three women. Two of them didn't seem too interested in his house. They would glance at it as they walked by, say something to each other and laugh, then just continue on. He hated the sound of their laughter. It worried him. But, that one woman, the shortest of the three, with the long, dark hair. She wouldn't just glance, she would stare! Sometimes he thought she might actually be able to see him, even though he knew it was impossible. She never laughed, and that worried him more.

During the past few years the foot traffic past his house had increased. At first he thought they might know, and he had felt panicky. Then, as he watched them go by, he realized that they were just following the latest health fad. He liked it better when people thought they had to run to stay in shape. Then they would run by quickly, and he felt safer. But now they walked. Some slower than others, but no one looked his way as they went by. These new ones were different. Especially the dark haired one. He would have to be careful.

He had lived in this house all of his life. When his parents had built it all those years ago, it was one of the few in this area. Back then the woods had stretched behind the house for miles, and it was his own private haven. He knew the woods so well, that even when other children played there he could watch them without being seen. How he hated those children.

He was a painfully shy, clumsy, and homely child. His parents were also very introverted, with no other family or friends, so they had little contact with other people. As a result, he distrusted and feared anyone other than his parents. Only once had he ever tried to play with the other children. He was about five years old at the time, and wanted to join in their game of Hide and Seek.

He was so shy that he found it hard to be with anyone other than his parents, let alone actually approach someone. They were older than he was and he was afraid, but they always looked like they were having so much fun, he finally forced himself to ask them if he could play. They let him join their game all right. He was so happy that he didn't even mind when they said that he had to be it.

They told him to lean against the tree, close his eyes, and count to 100.

He didn't know how to count to 100, but since he was too embarrassed to tell them, he stayed there counting to 10 over and over again, until he thought surely he had waited long enough. While he was counting, all of the children agreed to play a trick on him. It was time for them to go home for dinner anyway, so they would all just go home, and leave him there. What a funny joke that would be. When he started to look for them, he was sure he could find them all easily, because he knew the woods so well. But he looked everywhere, and he couldn't find any of them. He was terrified of the dark, but he was so worried about his new friends that even when darkness came, he still searched for them. When his parents finally came to find him, he was nearly hysterical, and tearfully told them the terrible news. All the children had disappeared.

His parents tried to reassure him that the children must have gone home, but he refused to believe them. They finally had to bring him to each of the children's homes to show him that they were all safe. That night he cried himself to sleep.

His parents had tried to comfort him, but he was inconsolable. He thought he had finally found some friends, and didn't understand why they had been so mean. His parents told him that he didn't need them, that they would take care of him, and protect him, but nothing could ease his pain. He spent the rest of the summer alone in his room, refusing to go outside.

The next time he saw the children was that September, when he started school for the first time. He thought that maybe they would be sorry for what they had done. Instead, they called him a baby for crying. They said that their parents had punished

14

them for their little joke, and it was all his fault. They told all the other children at school that he was a baby, and a troublemaker, and they should stay away from him. After that, he vowed that he would never let them hurt him again, and never let them make him cry.

He tried to keep to himself at school, but the other children always seemed to find new ways to torment him. They would tease him every chance they got, about the clothes he was wearing, the grades he was getting, his lack of athletic ability. He took it all, and held the tears and misery inside.

He spent most of his time outside of school alone, roaming his woods, hiding from the other children, and hating the sound of their laughter.

His parents were concerned for him, and worried about all the time he spent alone. They were afraid he blamed himself, and told him over and over that it wasn't him. It was them. Children could be so cruel. His parents loved him, but they were simple people, and had no idea what was happening in the mind of their only child. Except for meals, and when his mother would read aloud from the Bible, the only time he would really spend with his parents was when he would sit with them each night watching the evening news. His father would lament over the savageness in the world. "How can these people be so cruel?" he would say "They should be punished." He grew up hearing those same things, day after day. "Children are cruel." "Cruelty should be punished."

Eventually the children that lived around him grew up and moved away. But he stayed. His beloved woods were cleared away to make room for the new development, Eden Park. But he stayed. His parents grew old, and died within a year of each other. And still he stayed. Where else would he go?

The only places he ever felt safe and protected, were his woods and this house. His woods were gone, and all he had left was this house.

Because he had dropped out of school as soon as he could, he had little education, and the only job he could find was as a night watchman in a large warehouse. The job suited him though, because he had little contact with other people. He worked the third shift, and that suited him just fine. He would relieve the man on duty, with minimal conversation, and spend his eight-hour shift wandering the empty warehouse thinking about his other calling. The one that really mattered.

Even after his parents were gone, day after day he relived in his mind the only two lessons he could remember them teaching him. Children are cruel! Cruelty should be punished! How could his parents have ever known that his tortured mind would eventually merge the two thoughts until they became one?

Cruel Children Should Be Punished!

Chapter 5

When Rachel first moved to Eden Park she had set certain goals and standards for herself. She now lived in what she considered the perfect neighborhood so, naturally, she would be the perfect wife and mother, with the perfect family. She also decided that she would be friendly with her neighbors, but not become friends with them. She wanted to avoid the problems of fighting and jealousy that can so often develop when you become too close to your neighbors. But, that was not as easy as she thought.

Danny and Christie came over to introduce themselves shortly after the Palmer's moved in, and soon became permanent fixtures. They stopped over every day to visit, after Danny came home from work. They invited the Palmer's to their house every Saturday night to play cards, or watch videos. On the weekends, if Rachel and Michael were out in their yard playing ball with their kids, it wasn't long before Danny, Christie, and little Jimmy came over to join them. Christie even began to show up every morning to join Rachel and Sara for coffee. Sara would go home after about an hour, but Christie would stay until long after noontime.

Christie was the type of person who adjusted her personality, and life experiences, to conform to whomever she was trying to impress. Whatever little anecdote you might relate about something that had happened to you, Christie had experienced the exact same thing. If Rachel was upset with Michael about something, Christie was mad at her husband for the same reason. Rachel found this trait very annoying. She also resented the daily intrusions, but had no idea how to extricate herself from her newfound "best friend".

The only thing Christie never complained about was her sex life, because according to her, sex with Danny was the absolute best it could possibly be. This actually led Rachel to believe that sex might be the *only* problem that Christie and Danny really had.

Rachel's daily walks with Sara were one of the few times that she could relax, leave her family worries behind, and talk about anything that came into her head. When Christie began to invite herself along on these walks, Rachel's resentment of her intrusion into even this part of her life began to grow. She didn't want her along, but had no idea how to stop her without being cruel.

She supposed that was one of the reasons she was so vocal about the house on Rocky Ridge in front of Christie. She secretly hoped that Christie would get so nervous about it that she would eventually stay home. That's why she decided that when she finally talked to Sara seriously about what she was feeling, she intended to include Christie in the discussion. Besides, she hardly ever had a chance to talk to Sara alone anymore.

Chapter 6

Rachel decided that today would be the day she would talk to Sara and Christie. The hairs on the back of her neck were beginning to rise every time they walked by that house. She was starting to think that she was either getting some type of psychic vibration, or she was going crazy. She didn't really have a strong belief in the supernatural, but she couldn't completely discount it either. There were those incidents that had been happening in her own house that began shortly after her mother had died. She would tear the house apart looking for a particular sweater, and it would be nowhere to be found. The next day, she would find it draped across her bed, as though it was deliberately placed there. Sometimes her TV would go on and off on it's own too.

The music boxes were what finally convinced her that it was definitely connected to her mother. She had a collection of them in her bedroom, and one night when she was in bed watching TV, one of the music boxes dinged. It startled her, but she thought it must have just been some type of vibration in the house, when it happened again.

Suddenly, thoughts of her mother filled her head, and without really thinking about it, she said out loud "Ma, is that you?". The music box dinged again. Then she said "Ma, if that's you, I want you to prove it to me. I want you to ding the music box twice, not once-not three times-just twice." She waited a few minutes, but nothing happened.

Convinced that there was nothing strange going on after all, Rachel settled back down to watch TV. Then, about 10 minutes later, she heard "DING, DING". Although she felt a chill go up her back, she also felt excited and peaceful, at the same time. That was all the proof she needed that there really was something after you died, and it comforted her to know that her mother was still around. From that day on, Rachel never again scoffed at stories of paranormal happenings.

That was why when the hair on the back of her neck began to prickle, when she walked past that house, she really started to believe that she was picking up some kind of psychic vibration. She didn't know if she would relate that particular bit of information to Sara and Christie, but she was sure she would let them know that she was serious about something being wrong within that house.

The big problem was *how* to tell them, but the more immediate problem was *when*. She knew Sara would be over for coffee this morning, and whether she liked it or not, Christie would be there shortly after. She often wondered if Christie watched out her back door, waiting for Sara to get there, because she would always arrive a few minutes later. Rachel didn't know if she should do it this morning, or wait until their walk this evening. She would have to wait and see how the conversation went.

Sara arrived at 8:10 A.M., and true to form, Christie showed up at 8:15. Sara's big news of the morning was that Scott was taking the boys camping for the weekend. Her husband and sons loved camping, and Sara hated it. Her idea of a vacation was a beach in the daytime and a comfortable bed, a hot shower, and a color TV at night. Not fishing all day, and sleeping on the ground fighting bugs all night.

So Scott and the boys would go camping for a weekend, every once in while, and Sara would stay at home. Scott and the boys felt bad leaving her behind, but she assured them that she would be much happier at home.

Sara and Rachel had begun sort of a tradition, ever since Scott first took the boys camping overnight.

They would get a group of their girlfriends together, and have an old fashioned sleep over, with a slight variation. They all brought whatever alcoholic beverage they liked to drink, and since no one had to drive home, got totally wasted.

Since Scott and the boys were going to be gone this weekend, they decided that they would have one of their sleepovers that Friday night. Rachel thought that it would be the perfect time to bring up the house on Rocky Ridge, and she only had to wait one more day. Since Sara's house was located right behind that house, and they usually ended up out on the pool deck, it would be easy to turn the conversation in that direction.

With that decided, Rachel turned her attention to the headlines in the morning newspaper. Another child in the New England area had disappeared. That made three in the past few years. This time it was a 9-year-old girl, Amanda's age, named Missy Harper. She had been riding her bike up and down the street in front of her house, after school. When her mother went to call her in for dinner, she found her bike lying in the middle of the sidewalk, and nothing else.

The first child to disappear was a twelve year old girl, and the second a ten year old boy.

The newspaper article had said that since so much time had gone by between the other two disappearances, they had thought that they were totally unrelated, but with this third one the authorities were starting to wonder if they weren't connected. Rachel and Sara were extremely upset over the Harper girl's disappearance, and talked about how they had better start taking extra precautions with their own kids.

Since all the children who had disappeared were alone at the time, they decided that from then on they would only let their kids ride their bikes, if they were with two or more friends. They also decided that they wouldn't let them play outside alone at any time. They talked and worried, about this newest disappearance, and how it was hitting so close to home, because the children were the same ages as their own.

Christie, who's son Jimmy was only two, was apparently feeling a little left out, because she started to relay the story of how the exact same thing had happened when she was living in Ohio, only it was two year olds that were being taken. Rachel and Sara looked at each other and rolled their eyes. The silent communication of "Here she goes again".

Christie was born and raised in Crestwood, and the only time that she had lived anywhere else was the one year she lived in Ohio, after marrying Danny. As a result, whenever she talked about some event that would have been common knowledge if it had happened in Crestwood, it always seemed to have happened in Ohio. Rachel and Sara often marveled at the exciting life Christie must have lived during that year, because for all of her stories to be true, there must have been a monumental occurrence at least twice a week.

Chapter 7

He sat in his van at the side of the road, pretending to read a road map. He knew she would be along shortly, she usually rode her bike up and down this street after school. She was pretty, with long blond hair, and blue eyes. She had an innocent face that she could show to the world, whenever she thought anyone was watching, but he knew what she was really like. He had been following her for weeks, ever since that day in the park. He had followed Missy home that day, and for the next few weeks he watched her discreetly, from a distance. He stayed away from the school, because it was too risky. A grown man hanging around a schoolyard would not go unnoticed. So, he watched for her after school, and on the weekends.

He found out that the little boy he had seen at the park on that first day, lived only a few houses away from her. He saw him a few days later riding his bike in front of his house. He could tell Timmy was just learning to ride without training wheels, because he was still a little shaky.

Missy stood on the sidewalk, in front of her house, watching Timmy for a little while. Then she went around the back of her house, and came back with her bicycle. She rode back and forth in front of her house for a while, and then began to venture further and further, down the sidewalk toward Timmy.

The first time she past him she was far enough away, but he was so nervous, he almost fell. The second time she past him, she came even closer. He almost fell again, but caught himself just in time. The man heard Timmy say, "Hey, watch out you almost ran into me."

"It's not my fault if you can't even ride a two wheeler, maybe you better put the training wheels back on," Missy sneered.

The next time she headed right for him. Timmy was concentrating so much on his own riding that he didn't

23

see her coming. She reached out and shoved his bike as she went past. She did it so fast, that Timmy didn't even know what was happening. He went flying off his bike, and skidded down the sidewalk, scrapping both elbows.

As Timmy began to cry, the front door of his house opened, and his mother came running out. Missy immediately ran over to Timmy, and began to help him up. The man heard her telling Timmy's mother that he must have hit a rock or something, and lost his balance.

"I hope he's okay," Missy said. "Maybe he should still be using his training wheels."

"You may be right," said Timmy's mother, as she helped her sobbing son into the house.

The man saw Missy smiling as she picked up her bike, and headed back toward her own house. As he watched her for the next few weeks he saw similar incidents which showed him the true nature of this angelic looking little girl. While she appeared to have a lot of friends, and could be very nice to them, she seemed to take specific delight in her cruel treatment of this particular little boy. He finally made his decision, which brought him to where he was today.

He had stopped at the animal shelter earlier in the day, and picked out the tiniest, cutest little puppy they had. Publicity about child abductions had taught him that a man looking for a lost puppy was one of the best devices used to lure children. His own experience had taught him that having a cute little puppy, and looking for the owner, worked even better. It seemed that the one thing most children, even the cruelest ones, couldn't resist was a puppy. It also could be used as the perfect cover story, should any adults suddenly appear.

As soon as Missy began to venture further from her own house, and was directly across the street from his van, the man got out, went around the back, and opened the door. He took the puppy out of the back, and said,

"*Excuse me, do you know of anyone who may have lost a puppy?*"

Missy stopped, looked over at the man, and asked, "*Are you talking to me?*"

"*I'm sorry to bother you,*" the man said. "*But I found this poor little puppy, and I am trying to find the owner. Have you ever seen him before?*"

He held the puppy in his arms, so that only the tip of his snout was visible.

Missy hesitated, but she really wanted to see the puppy. Maybe she would even say it was hers. She put her bike down, and walked slowly across the street. As she got nearer to the van, the man reached inside, and put the puppy into a box in the back.

"*He's getting awfully squirmy, and I don't want to drop him,*" he said.

Missy came up to the back of the van, looked inside the box, and saw the most adorable puppy she'd ever seen. All of her attention was on the puppy, and she forgot about the man completely.

In what seemed like one motion, the man put his hand over Missy's mouth, scooped her into the van, and closed the door. Once inside, he opened a can containing a moist cloth, and held it over Missy's nose and mouth for a few seconds, until Missy's body went limp. As a precaution, he tied her hands and feet, and gagged her mouth. Then he got into the driver's seat, and slowly drove away, whistling. The only other sound, was the whining of a hungry little puppy.

Chapter 8

Rachel and Sara always looked forward to their "sleepovers" with the anticipation of adolescents. Since day after day they had to be responsible for their families and homes, it was like having one night with absolutely no responsibilities, and they loved it. They planned what they would have to eat and drink down to the smallest detail. They went through dozens of video titles to pick the scariest ones they could find to rent, even though at least two out of three of their choices always seemed to turn out to be the worst movies they'd ever seen.

This time there would be four of them altogether, Rachel, Sara, Christie, and Jenna. They had invited two other friends, but they weren't going to be able to make it. They wondered if there would still be four of them in the morning, because the last time Christie had gone home before midnight.

She said that her back had been bothering her, and she had to sleep in her own bed. Rachel and Sara suspected that Danny wouldn't agree to her spending the night, and Christie could never admit that Rachel was able to do something that she couldn't.

As far as Rachel was concerned, the guest list was perfect. She desperately wanted to discuss the house on Rocky Ridge, and now she was sure she would be able to. Other than Rachel and Christie, Jenna had been the only other person she had ever mentioned the house to. She had told her that there was this house in her neighborhood that was really spooky looking, and Jenna had told her that one of these days she had to show it to her. Since Jenna and Rachel had been friends since they were children, she knew she would be able to speak her mind. She hoped that the three women would either be able to convince her that her feelings were unfounded, or together they could come up with some plan of action.

All day Thursday and Friday, Rachel would constantly find herself going over in her mind how she would bring up the subject, and what she was going to

say. She even looked for movies at the video store
that might involve a similar situation, so that she
could ease into the conversation. The only one she
found was one that involved a neighbor that was
actually a murderer. She could tell by the completely
unknown actors that it would probably be a terrible
movie, but she rented it anyway.

By six o'clock on Friday, everyone was at Sara's
except for Christie. They figured she had to get
Jimmy bathed and ready for bed before she could leave.
Jenna had met Christie on a couple of other occasions,
and was telling Rachel and Sara that she didn't know
how they handled dealing with her all the time.

"I really don't have to," said Sara. "When it gets
too much for me, I conveniently have other things to
do at home."

"Well tonight you won't be able to escape, will
you?" Rachel laughed.

"No, but at least I won't be all alone with her."
Sara teased.

"I really don't know if I'm going to be able to
control myself if she starts telling another 'The
exact same thing happened to me' story," said Jenna.

"Jenna, if you start that uncontrollable giggling
again, I'm going to kill you," threatened Rachel.

"Hey, you know how I am, and you invited me anyway,
so I'm not making any promises," Jenna countered.

"You know what we should do?" Sara interjected.
"We should make up a really off the wall story, and
see what she does. Jenna, she hardly knows you, so
you should be the one to do it."

"That would be great," said Jenna "But, I don't
know if I can pull it off without starting to laugh
halfway through it."

"Don't you dare," said Rachel.

"What we have to do is make it something really
simple," said Sara, ignoring Rachel's protest. "I'VE
GOT IT!" she cried. "Jenna, remember the time your
daughter was missing? You searched everywhere, and
even called the police, and they found her asleep

27

under her own bed. That would be perfect, because it's true, so you wouldn't have to try to remember what to say."

"You guys are so bad," said Rachel, laughing. "But this really could be funny."

"We should make bets on who it's going to be that had the 'exact same thing' happen to them." said Sara. "Her sister, her brother, her aunt, her uncle, or the ever popular Christie herself."

"I'll take Christie," said Rachel. "It's much more dramatic that way."

"Me too," Jenna and Sara said simultaneously. Just then the doorbell rang.

"Heads up you guys," said Sara, looking out of the window. "Our last guest has arrived."

Sara went to answer the door, and Jenna immediately started to giggle.

"Oh great!" Rachel said. "She's not even in the door yet, and you're starting already."

"I'll be good, I promise," said Jenna, as she started laughing again. Unable to avoid Jenna's contagious laughter, Rachel started laughing herself. When Sara and Christie walked into the room, Jenna and Rachel were laughing so hard tears were rolling down their cheeks.

"What's so funny?" Christie asked.

"Yeah, what did we miss?" asked Sara, with a mischievous glint in her eye. "Don't keep us in suspense."

"Oh, you know Jenna," Rachel was finally able to say. "She starts laughing about absolutely nothing, and can't stop."

"Something must have gotten her started," pressed Sara. "Come on, let us in on it."

"Let's make some drinks," Rachel said, changing the subject, and kicking Jenna under the table.

Sara decided to let them off the hook, and steering Christie into the kitchen, asked her if she wanted to try one of the new summer sensation drinks they had invented.

Chapter 9

His first stop was the animal shelter.   After holding the chloroform soaked rag to the unconscious Missy's nose for a few seconds, just as an extra precaution, he took the puppy inside.   He was very apologetic, but his landlord would not let him have a dog.   Yes, he was disappointed, because it was such a cute puppy, but he was sure someone else would adopt it.

He really did feel sad leaving the cute little bundle of fur behind, but the last thing he needed was an animal that might draw attention to him.   His dogs were easy enough to care for, and if anything they kept people away from his house.   A puppy would need much more care, and if anyone saw him with it, they might actually approach him.

He drove around for the next few hours, waiting for it to get dark.   He needed the darkness to get Missy into the house.   While he drove, he thought of his past mistakes, and how to avoid them this time.   He knew it was his mission to punish the cruel children, but he never actually meant for them to die.   The other two were mistakes, not his fault at all.

If he thought about it, it was really their own fault.

They were supposed to have learned their lesson, but they fought him all the way.   If they had just acted the way they were supposed to, they would have been all right, but no-they had to fight him.   Now, their lifeless bodies were beneath the murky waters of Eden Pond.

When it happened the first time he was in a panic. What was he going to do now?   At first he thought, he hoped, that she had just fainted or something.   But then when he shook her, he saw the blood.   So much blood.   He sat and watched her for hours, but she never moved.   Finally, he had to face the fact that she was dead.   The disappointment of his failure was overwhelming.   He thought of bringing her home, leaving her in front of her house, and letting someone else take care of it. But he was too afraid that someone might see him. Then he remembered Eden Pond.

It used to be a recreation area, where families used to picnic and swim, but that was a long time ago. Before the water became polluted, and the city closed it down for health reasons. Now it was a huge body of murky water, where no one went. Some of the kids in the area still played on the grassy hills there, but even they wouldn't go near the water. Not with the poisonous snakes slithering in and out. He had wrapped her body securely in an old tarp, weighted it down with cinder blocks, and dumped it into the deepest section of Eden Pond. When it happened the second time, he felt the same deep disappointment, but no panic. He knew just what to do with his failure, and vowed to keep on trying until he got it right.

The sun had finally set, and as luck would have it, it was a cloudy moon less night. It was only late May, but it was hot and muggy, and the humidity was oppressive. He pulled around the back, carried the still unconscious Missy into the house, and brought her down to the cellar.

He had taken great pains to create the perfect setting for his work. The room was completely soundproof. The walls and ceiling were plaster, none of that flimsy sheet rock. The lights were recessed into the ceiling, with metal grates covering them. The floor was cement, with a large rug in the middle. There was a toilet and sink in the corner, with a divider separating them from the rest of the room. The divider rested six inches off the floor, and was four feet high. There was one small window near the ceiling, covered with a heavy dark material. The only "furniture" was a dirty mattress on the floor, and a worn and scared wooden chair.

As he laid Missy on the mattress, he was so anxious to get started, that he considered sitting there and waiting for her to wake up. But, from his past experience he knew that she would be asleep for hours.

Reluctantly, he left the room, closed the insulated steel door, and turned the key that slid the dead bolt into place. He had been sure to buy the kind of lock that needed a key from both sides. That way, he could lock the door securely, even when he was inside the room. He came down twice to check on her, but she was still unconscious. He wished he didn't have to go to work, because he wanted to be there as soon as she woke up. Now that he had her here, the anxiety he always experienced once he had made a selection vanished. As he left for work the only feeling he experienced, was an actual tingling of anticipation to get started.

Missy turned over. The first sensation she had was a pounding in her head, which was followed quickly by a dryness in her mouth and throat. She had no idea where she was, but she knew it wasn't her bed. The blanket was rough and scratchy, not at all like her silky comforter. And the bed was hard, lumpy, and it smelled bad. She started to sit up, but her head hurt too much.

Where was she, and how did she get here? The last thing she remembered was riding her bike, and Timmy falling off of his. Well, he didn't actually *fall* off, but he would have sooner or later. At least that was one thing she could do better than him. His mother was always bragging about how smart he was, and how he never got anything but straight A's on his report cards. Missy wanted her parents to be just as proud of her, but no matter how hard she tried, she just couldn't get those kinds of grades. It was just so easy for him, and even though he never made a big deal out it, she hated him for it.

She tried to sit up again, and this time despite the pain, she made it. There was a covered window way up near the ceiling, and the daylight coming in around the edges was just enough for her to see the room she was in. As she looked around, she was sure that she had never been here before. The room was big, but the only things in it were a chair, a dirty sink and toilet, and the mattress she was sitting on. There was also a large dark stain on the edge of the floor, near the wall. She thought this had to be a very bad dream. There was no way she could actually be in a place like this. She laid down again, and closed her eyes. She had to get back to sleep, because if she did, she knew that the next time she woke up she would be back in her own bed. "Please God, let me wake up in my own bed." she prayed.

As soon as he got home, he rushed down to the cellar to see if she was awake. As he walked into the room, he thought he saw her move, but when he checked closer she was still sleeping. He was disappointed, but knew that he had to let her wake up on her own. When he had tried to force them awake before, they were too groggy to even understand what he was saying.

He went back upstairs, and tried to forget that she was there, but all he could think about was how cruel she was. He was sure that he would be able to succeed with this one. All he had to do was slow down, and control his temper.

He realized now that with the others he had moved too fast. He had expected them to be sorry right away for what they were, and when they weren't it had made him furious. This time would be different. This time he would take his time. He didn't think he could stand another failure.

The next time he checked on her, she was just waking up. It had been more than 36 hours since he had first taken her, and he knew she would be hungry and thirsty by now.

He brought her a peanut butter sandwich, and a glass of milk.

She was sitting against the wall with her arms wrapped around her knees. She ignored the plate and glass he placed on the floor, looked at him, and asked timidly, "Who are you?"

He just stared at her, and didn't answer. As she looked at him closely, a look of surprise came over her face, and she said, "You're the man with the lost puppy. Where am I? How did I get here? Where is the puppy? Did you find his owner?"

"Oh, you care so much about an animal," he sneered. "But when it comes to an innocent little boy, you don't care at all do you?"

The tone in his voice made Missy shrink back closer against the wall, as she barely whispered, "What are you talking about?"

The man stood silently for a minute, trying to get his temper under control.

"I'm taking about Timmy," he answered quietly. "The little boy that you love to torture. That's very cruel, and you know something Missy, Cruel Children Should Be Punished."

With that, he turned and left the room.

Missy pulled her knees up tighter under chin, and began to cry. This isn't a nightmare, she thought. This is real, and much worse than any nightmare I have ever had in my life.

Chapter 10

While Sara and Christie were busy in the kitchen, Rachel said to Jenna, "Now get control of yourself. This is never going to work if you can't even talk."

I'm okay now, but I can't promise that I won't get started again. When she tells us about 'the same thing happening to her', I'm going to lose it. I just know it."

"Well, maybe we'd better call the whole thing off."

"No way, I have to see if she will really say it. I'll try to control myself, just don't look at me."

"Okay, but I'm really starting to think this is a bad idea."

Just then, Sara and Christie came into the room, with drinks for everyone. They all talked about what had been happening with Jenna since they saw her last, then they went on to complain about the little things their husband's did that irritated them, and finally they began to talk about their kids. Rachel talked about how Amanda and Brian were always fighting, and how she wished she knew how make them get along better.

"Amanda can be such a little witch that, as horrible as it sounds, sometimes I don't even like her."

"Rachel we all feel like that sometimes, and I hate to sound like a parenting magazine, but it's not really our kids that we don't like, it the things they do." Sara offered, and then asked. "Is she like that with everyone, or just Brian?"

"Now that I think about it, I guess it *is* just Brian. She has a lot of friends, and gets along really well with them. It's just her brother that she's always mean to."

"Maybe she feels that Brian has taken you away from her," Jenna offered.

"You know, that could be true," Sara agreed. "Amanda was your 'Little Princess' for almost three years, and then 'The Prince' came along and everything changed."

"But I never gave her any reason to think that I thought Brian was better, or more important than her," Rachel said, defensively.

"Rachel, you don't have to give a child a reason to feel that way. Just the fact that you have to spend so much time with a new baby could be enough," said Jenna.

"And then when they start acting horrible, and we react to that, it makes them feel it all the more," Sara added.

"Well, now that I've totally screwed up my daughter's life, what do you suggest?"

"Rachel don't be so defensive," Jenna chided. "No one said you screwed up her life."

That's right" said Sara "And believe me, you're not alone. After Joey was born, Taran would have these crying fits. When I'd ask him what was wrong, he would look at me and say 'You just know!'. I had no idea what to do about it."

"Being a parent is scary," Jenna agreed, "because you just don't have all the answers. I guess we really *could* screw up our kids, but we just have to do the best we can, and hope it's enough."

"Well, I must be doing something wrong," Rachel sighed, "because Amanda is so mean to Brian that sometimes I'd just like to ship her off somewhere."

"RACHEL!" scolded Sara. "You know you don't mean that. If anything ever happened to Amanda, you'd die."

"That's right," Jenna added, as she winked at Sara. "Look at what happened to me when I thought Michelle was lost."

Christie, who had been uncharacteristically, quiet during their discussion about raising siblings, asked, "What happened?"

Jenna relayed the story about thinking her daughter was lost, only to have the police discover her asleep under her own bed. True to form, Christie said that the same thing had happened to her when she was a little girl, but she was asleep in her closet. Of course in Christie's case, she was missing for hours, and practically the whole city was searching for her. Even though they had expected it, Rachel, Sara, and Jenna were still amazed. This woman was literally, unbelievable.

Fortunately for them, the doorbell rang, and Sara said "I guess the pizza is here."

Sometimes, at these gatherings, they would prepare elaborate meals complete with appetizers and dessert, but tonight they had decided to make it easy on themselves, and order pizza. After they had finished eating, Rachel asked if everyone was ready to watch a movie.

"What did you get?" Jenna asked.

"I hope it's not too scary," Christie said.

"Don't worry, Christie," Sara laughed. "The movies we get are supposed to be scary, but usually just end up being stupid."

Rachel didn't care what the movie was like. All she knew was that it was about a neighbor, who was really a murderer.

As they watched the movie, which really was one of the worse they had ever seen, Rachel waited for an opportunity to bring up the house on Rocky Ridge.

Finally there was a scene where the heroine was trying to convince a police detective that her neighbor had killed someone. The detective scoffed at her, saying, "That kind of thing just doesn't happen in a nice suburban neighborhood like this. I think you're letting your imagination get away from you."

"Did you hear that?" asked Rachel. "What if something like that were going on right here in this neighborhood, and no one did anything because they thought it just couldn't happen here?"

"Oh no," groaned Christie.

"What are you talking about?" asked Jenna.

"She's talking about that house on Rocky Ridge, again," answered Christie. "And I don't want to hear about it."

"If you don't think there is something strange about that place, why do you get so upset whenever I mention it?" Rachel questioned.

"What place are you talking about?" Jenna asked, again.

"Remember that house I told you about that has been giving me the creeps?"

"Oh, I *do* remember you talking about that. You promised to show it to me the next time I was up here."

"NO!" cried Christie. "Jenna, you don't know what you're asking for. Rachel is totally obsessed with that place."

"I'll tell you what," Sara suggested. "Let's go in the pool first. It's so hot and muggy tonight, I think we could all use a swim. Then, we'll talk about what to do after that."

Everyone, even Christie, agreed. They changed into their suits, and Sara fixed more drinks to bring out to the pool deck. They all splashed around in the cool water, laughed at Jenna's water ballet routine, and the house on Rocky Ridge was forgotten for a while. Later, as they sat on the deck, sipping their drinks and enjoying the warm night breeze, Rachel looked across the back of Sara's yard, and saw the dark house looming in the distance.

"Sara, have you ever even seen anyone over there?" she asked.

"No, never," Sara answered.

"And, you don't consider that strange?"

"Maybe no one even lives there," Christie suggested, hopefully.

"Oh, and I suppose those dogs that we always hear just feed themselves," Rachel answered, sarcastically.

"Sara, have you ever looked over your fence to see if you can see anything," Jenna asked.

"Of course not," Sara answered.   "That would be just too, too, I don't know what."

"Probably illegal," offered Christie.

"Sara, I have to tell you the truth," Rachel confessed. "I know that you think I've been kidding around about that house, but I really think something bad is going on in there."

"What makes you think that?" Jenna asked.

"I can't explain it, but the feeling I get is so strong that I just can't ignore it anymore.   Maybe I *have* just let my imagination get away from me, but I have to find out."

Sara looked at Rachel for a long time.   She had known this woman for years.   She knew that Rachel could be really dramatic sometimes, and she did have a wild imagination, but this wasn't curiosity she saw on her face, it was fear.   Sara didn't know if the fear she saw was caused by her feelings about the house or because she was afraid of what everyone might think of her, but because of that look, Sara made a decision.

"I guess it won't hurt to take a look," she said.

"You can't be serious!" exclaimed Christie.

"Oh Christie, don't be such a baby," Sara laughed. "We're not going to do anything illegal, just take a look over my own fence."

"You can stay here if you want to," Rachel suggested.

"Oh all right, I'll go," Christie said. "But I still don't like it."

"Let's go then," Sara said.   "The fence is about eight feet tall, so we'll have to get a ladder out of the shed."

Chapter 11

After his outburst, he had left her alone for the rest of the day, and that night. He had wanted to give her time to think about what he had said, and to give himself time to get his temper under control. It enraged him every time he thought about her asking about that stupid animal, and he had to be sure he could control that rage.

He had gone out that day, driving around the city, stopping at numerous garage sales. He finally found what he was looking for, loaded it into his van, and took it home.

He waited until after dark again, so that no one would see him bringing it into the house. When he finally went down to Missy, he was confident that it would be a productive session.

As he walked in, and locked the door behind him, he noticed that she was awake, and sitting in the chair.

"You had better let me out of here, or you're going to be in big trouble," she said, defiantly.

"I think you might be the one in big trouble," he said menacingly, and was happy to see the look of fear spread over her face.

"What are you going to do?" she asked, her eyes wide with fear.

"I'M GOING TO SHOW YOU WHAT IT'S LIKE TO BE A LITTLE BOY, AND HAVE CRUEL CHILDREN TORTURE YOU, OVER AND OVER AGAIN, UNTIL YOU WISH YOU COULD WIPE THEM ALL OFF THE FACE OF THE EARTH," he shouted.

He knew he was losing control again, and that he had to calm down. He heard his dogs start to bark, and then quiet down right away. It was probably just a stray cat, or a skunk, but he thought he had better go out and check anyway.

Missy began to cry when she heard the dead bolt slide into place. She knew she was in trouble now. This guy was crazy, and from the way his eyes had looked when he had screamed at her, she knew that he was dangerous too. He had something planned for her, something bad, and she had to get out of here. She tried the door, but as she knew it would be, it was locked. She walked around the edge of the room, looking for some other opening, but there was none. She looked at the window and knew, even if she stood on the chair, she could never reach it. It was hopeless. He was going to hurt her, and there was nothing she could do about it.

"Please help me," she whispered. "Someone help me."

He went over to the dog pens, and looked around. The dogs were quiet now. The lights around the pool were on, in the yard behind him, but there was no one outside. He knew one of the women who walked with the dark haired one lived there. He had seen them swimming, and having cookouts with their families. But everything seemed quiet over there now.

He walked back to his house, glancing back towards Sara's house, every couple of steps. He would have to watch them more closely now, he decided. That dark haired woman still made him nervous.

When he came back into the house, he went into the living room, and sat down. He had to make sure he was perfectly calm before he went down to Missy again. He was afraid that if he lost control, he would make a mistake again, and have to start all over. When he was sure he felt calm enough, he got up, took the bicycle he had bought at the garage sale, and brought it down to the cellar. It was time for Missy to learn her lesson. He brought it into the room, and put it in the middle of the floor.

"What's that for?" Missy asked.

"It's for you," he said, smiling. "You like to ride bikes, don't you?"

"But, that's a boy's bike, and it's way too big for me."

"Well, Timmy was riding a boy's bike, wasn't he? And considering how small he was, I'd say this bike is just perfect for you."

"Are we going outside?" she asked, hopefully.

"No, I think you'll do fine right here," he said, still smiling.

"I can't do it," she said.

"Well I think you'd better try," he said, raising his voice.

Missy was afraid of what he would do if she refused again, so she got up, and went over to the bike. She picked it up, and swinging her leg over the bar, sat on it. It was so big that she had to stand on the very tips of her toes to reach the floor.

"I told you it was too big for me," she moaned.

"RIDE IT!" he commanded.

Missy was so startled that she fell over, and the bike landed on her leg. As she started to cry, he started to laugh, and asked, "What's the matter? Does falling off of a bike hurt? You don't know anything about being hurt yet, but you will."

Just then, his dogs began to bark more furiously than he had ever heard before. Someone was out there. He rushed out, slammed the door, and quickly turned the key. As he rushed up the stairs, he never realized that he had turned the key in the wrong direction, and the dead bolt did not slide into place.

Chapter 12

Rachel and Sara got the ladder out of the shed, and headed for the back fence. Jenna was right behind them, and Christie trailed a few feet back. It was dark in the back part of Sara's property, but the lights from around the pool illuminated it just enough for them to see where they were going. They placed the ladder against the fence, and Rachel immediately climbed to the top. Sara followed her up, and squeezed in next to her, so they could both see over the fence. Jenna climbed part way up, and Christie stayed at the bottom, looking around nervously.

It was much darker on the other side of the fence, but light enough to make out shadows and shapes. As Rachel looked over the fence, the first thing she noticed was a dark van, parked near the back door.

"See, I told you someone lives there," she whispered to Sara.

"I don't think I've ever seen that van before," Sara whispered back.

"Look!" Rachel whispered, urgently. "There's a light. You can barely see it around the edges of the cellar window."

"That *is* kind of strange," Sara answered. "No lights anywhere in the house, except the cellar."

"What are you two talking about? Do you see anything?" Jenna asked, a little too loudly.

"Can we get out of here now?" Christie asked, *much* too loudly.

At that moment, the dogs on the other side of the fence started barking. Rachel, Sara, and Jenna scrambled down the ladder, knocking Christie over at the bottom. Sara pulled the ladder down, laid it flat on the ground next to the fence, and they all ran back to the house.

As they gathered in the living room, Rachel said to Christie, "I hope you never decide to go into the spy business, you'd never make it."

"Trust me, the thought never entered my mind," Christie replied.

"So did you get a chance to see anything?" Jenna asked.

"Not much," answered Sara. "There's a van parked near the back door, and light showing from one of the cellar windows."

"That doesn't sound too suspicious to me," Christie said.

Rachel looked at Christie, and said, "You'd say that even if we saw bodies lined up across the back yard."

"And you would think it was strange if you saw nothing at all," replied Christie, defensively.

"Well, I do happen to think it's unusual that there's a van there that Sara and I have never seen before, and that the only light in the whole house, is coming from the cellar."

"What should we do now?" asked Jenna.

"I think we need some exercise. Why don't we go for a walk," Rachel answered.

"By any chance were you thinking of walking down, oh Rocky Ridge, for example," Sara teased.

"Not me!" Christie insisted. "I'll stay right here, thank you very much."

"I'll go," said Jenna.

"Me too, but don't get too daring, Rachel," Sara warned "I don't want Scott to have to bail me out of jail when he gets home."

"Okay, I promise, now let's get ready to go," Rachel said.

The three women changed out of their bathing suits, and headed for the door. Rachel turned to Christie, and said,

"If you change your mind, you can catch up to us. You know where we'll be."

"Yeah, in big trouble," Christie said, under her breath.

As the three women walked towards Rocky Ridge, they were all lost in their own thoughts. Jenna was excited, thinking of this as an adventure. She didn't really think that they would see anything sinister. They would just walk past the house, talk about how creepy it looked, and then go back to Sara's house and forget it.

Sara's thoughts were on Rachel. She had never seen her friend like this before. She was so determined to find out more about the house, and whoever lived there. She didn't know what was driving Rachel, but she was just as determined to stick by her, and not let her go through this alone.

Rachel was thinking only about the house. She knew she had promised Sara that she would not be too daring, but she really wanted to get a closer look. The window she had seen the light coming from was at the corner of the house. Maybe she would be able to get close enough to see something through the window.

As they approached the house, Jenna asked, "So what are we going to do? Just walk by, or what?"

"That's the plan," replied Sara. "Right Rachel?"

"Let's stop behind those bushes for a minute," Rachel said.

"All right, but just for a minute," Sara insisted.

As they crouched behind the bushes, Sara knew this was not going to be good enough for Rachel, and she was right.

"I'll be right back," Rachel said, suddenly.

Before anyone could stop her, she ran around the bushes, and up to the side of the house. Now that she was actually next to the house, the feelings that Rachel had been experiencing were even stronger. She was so scared, but now that she was this close, she had to try to see in the window.

"What is she doing?" whispered Jenna.

"Just what I was afraid she would do," groaned Sara. "She's going to try to look in the window."

"Is she crazy?" Jenna gasped. "What if she gets caught? Or attacked by those dogs?"

Rachel crept silently along the side of the house, careful to stay below the edge of the first floor windows. Just because there was no light coming from them didn't mean that there wasn't someone watching from the darkness. As she reached the corner of the house, she stopped to catch her breath. She was almost there. All she had to do was get around the corner, to the window.

As she crawled around the corner, and was almost to the window, the dogs started barking furiously. She hadn't realized how close the dogs were to the house, but when she looked up she could see them. There were three rottweilers barking, snarling, and trying to get through the fencing of their pens. Rachel stood up, and ran as fast as she could back to Sara and Jenna.

"What happened?" Jenna asked, breathlessly.

Ignoring Jenna's question, Rachel said, "Let's get out of here, NOW!"

The three women raced back to Sara's house, looking behind them every few minutes, sure that someone would be chasing them. When they got back to Sara's house, they noticed a note taped to the back door.

Dear Rachel, Sara, and Jenna,

Danny called and said that Jimmy woke up with a nightmare, and he couldn't get him back to sleep, because he wanted his Mommy. Sorry to bail on you, but since I had to go home anyway, I figured I'd just sleep there. Thanks for inviting me. It was fun.

Love,
Christie

"Well we wondered what the excuse would be this time," Rachel said. "My guess is that she just didn't want to be here when we got back."

"Guess what, guys," Sara said, as she came back from the living room. "According to my Caller ID, no one called from Christie's house."

Rachel ran her fingers through her hair, and said, "Oh my God!"

What's the matter?" Jenna asked.

"My hair bow!" she exclaimed. "It's gone."

"Gone? Gone where?" Sara asked.

"I remember putting it back in my hair when I changed out of my suit. I must have lost it when we went for the walk."

"You mean you could have dropped it when you were sneaking around that house?" Sara asked, alarmed.

I guess so," Rachel admitted. "But don't worry, it's not like it has my name on it, or anything."

"What happen back there, Rachel?" Sara asked with concern.

"I'm sorry Sara," Rachel apologized. "I know I said I wouldn't do anything stupid, but I couldn't help myself."

"So what did you see?" Jenna asked.

"Nothing. I was almost to the window when those dogs started up again. They were so close, I could see them snarling. It's a good thing their pens were strong, or I would have been ripped apart."

"What are you going to do now?" Jenna asked.

"I don't know. The dogs are really caged in tight. If it wasn't that I was afraid of someone catching me, I would have been able to look around. Maybe I'll just have to wait until the van isn't there."

Sara was afraid to say anything. She didn't want Rachel to know that she wanted to stop her, because then she might try to do it on her own. If she just let her think that she would go along with her, maybe she could talk her out of it when the time came.

"Well, there's nothing we can do about it tonight, because we know someone *is* there," she said, "so let's try to get some sleep."

Sara and Jenna slept fitfully that night. Jenna dreamed that dogs were chasing her, and Sara dreamed that they were attacking Rachel, while she watched helplessly.

Rachel didn't sleep well either. The fear she had experienced that night was something she had never felt before. She tried to convince herself that she was being ridiculous. That it was just an ordinary house, that happened to look a little different. That

46

whoever lived there, just liked to keep to himself, and not be bothered by anyone. When she finally did fall asleep, she dreamt of her mother. Her mother was telling her to be careful, that her family was in danger, and she had to stop him before it was too late. She didn't remember the dream when she woke up, and attributed the fear she still felt to the events of the previous night.

Chapter 13

As soon as he went out the door, Missy waited to hear the dead bolt slide into place. She didn't hear it. Maybe she just wasn't listening closely enough. She was afraid to move. Afraid to get her hopes up, and then find out that the door really was locked. Then she thought about him, and the last thing he had said. *"You don't know anything about being hurt yet, but you will."* She knew that she had to try to get away.

She stood up, and moved painfully to the door. Her leg, where the bike had fallen on it, hurt a lot but she kept moving. She turned the handle, and pulled on the door. To her surprise, it opened.

He rushed outside, and went immediately to the dog pens. The dogs had stopped barking, but they were still agitated. They paced up an down, whining. He heard something that sounded like footsteps on the other side of the house, and ran quickly around to the front. He looked toward the street, and thought he saw movement near the bushes lining the front of his property.

When he got to the edge of his front yard, he looked down the street, and saw three figures running around the corner.

Missy limped slowly through the door, and looked around. It was worse out here than it was inside the room, darker and creepier, but her fear made her keep moving. She found the stairs, and climbed them slowly, expecting him to appear at the top any minute. The door at the top was open, and she found herself in the kitchen. She saw the back door, and started to open it when she heard dogs whining. From the sounds they were making she knew they were big dogs, and they sounded very close. She decided not to take the chance that they might be right outside the door, and moved through the kitchen into the living room.

In the dim light, she could make out an old couch, a chair, and a small television in the corner. Then she spotted the front door, and limped quickly towards it. As she was about to open the door, she heard him coming back into the house, through the back door. She quickly moved to the chair, and crouched down behind it.

As he came into the house, he was thinking that the people he saw were probably just making so much noise when they ran past the house, that they excited the dogs.

Although he knew he should give himself time to calm down, he immediately headed for the cellar, and Missy. As he got to the bottom of the stairs, he realized that the flashlight he was carrying wasn't necessary, because there was light coming from somewhere. Then he saw the door to his special room standing open. He rushed into the room, and found it empty. How could she have gotten out? He was sure he had locked the door. But she definitely wasn't here, and now everything was ruined. Wait a minute, he thought, If she had gotten outside, he would have seen her. She must still be in the house, but she could be escaping this very minute, while I'm down here.

"NOOOOO!" he screamed, as he rushed back up the stairs.

Missy, was still hiding behind the chair, when she heard him scream. The sound sent a chill down her spine, and paralyzed her with fear. She couldn't decide what to do, stay hidden, or run for the door. When she heard him coming up the stairs, she panicked, and scrambled for the door. She turned the handle and pulled, but it wouldn't open.

She pulled, and pulled, and couldn't understand why it wouldn't open, until she noticed the lock. As she fumbled to unlock the door, he raced into the room.

As he came into the room, he saw Missy frantically trying to open the door. He lunged for her, grabbed her by the hair, and dragged her through the house. As they reached the kitchen, he stood her up, and pushed her towards the cellar stairs.

"Oh no you don't," he said. "I'm not finished with you yet. I have a lot more work to do."

Missy collapsed on the floor, crying hysterically. This enraged him even more. He stood her up again, and pushed her violently through the doorway. Missy's tiny body sailed through the doorway, and tumbled down the stairs, landing in a heap at the bottom.

He stood at the top of the stairs in shock. This can't be happening, not again. He stood there for a while waiting to see her move, listening for her to make some sound, but she was quiet and still. As he walked slowly down the stairs, he thought, I bet she's just faking. She's really good at faking.

Look how she could pretend to be such a nice little girl, when she was really so mean and cruel. As he got to the bottom of the stairs, he saw the blood spreading across the floor. He sat down next to Missy, as the familiar feeling of failure overcame him.

"Why?" he whispered. "Why did this have to happen? I was being so careful to control my temper. I made sure I didn't go too fast. I was doing everything right. If only you hadn't tried to get away."

"YOU RUINED EVERYTHING!" he screamed at Missy's lifeless body.

He sat there for a long time, unable to shake the unbearable disappointment. He was so sure he would succeed this time. So sure that he would do it right.

Eventually, he forced himself to get up. He had to stop feeling sorry for himself, and move on. He got the tarp, the rope, and the cinder blocks he would need. Eden Pond would claim another failure, and he would begin his search again. He promised himself that he would not give up. he couldn't, no matter how much the failures hurt. He had to keep trying. If he *didn't, there wouldn't be anyone to make them pay for the torture and misery innocent children had to endure. Innocent children like Timmy, and himself.*

Chapter 14

The next morning Rachel, Sara and Jenna sat around Sara's kitchen table, drinking coffee, and talking about the previous night's events. At first they just laughed about the fun they had in the pool, acting like silly kids. Then they marveled at how predictable Christie's behavior had been. Rachel said, "I wonder if I'll have the nerve to ask her how Danny got in touch with her, since we know he didn't use the telephone."

"I don't mean to sound petty," Sara responded. "But, I really think it's about time someone started calling her on her lies. It was funny at first, but now it's really starting to get to me."

"Me too," Rachel agreed. "But, I'm such a coward that I probably won't say a word."

"You didn't seem like such a coward last night," Jenna disagreed.

Sara groaned inwardly. She was hoping they could put off talking about their escapade for a few days. She thought that might give Rachel enough time to realize how foolish she had been. But, here was Jenna giving Rachel the perfect opportunity to talk about formulating a new plan of action.

To her surprise, Rachel said, "No, I wasn't a coward, I was just plain stupid. I can't believe I did that. If I ever got caught, the least of my worries would have been being accused of being a 'Peeping Tom'. If there really is something bad happening there, I could have been killed."

"If?" questioned Sara.

"I know I was thoroughly convinced last night, but in the cold light of day, and now that I'm sober, I'm not so sure."

Sara breathed a sigh of relief, and said, "Well, I don't think anyone saw us, so there was no harm done."

"Thank God for that." Rachel answered, sullenly.

"Hey, it's supposed to be a beautiful day tomorrow, why don't we have a barbecue here," Sara said, changing the subject. "I know Scott and the boys will be bringing home plenty of fish, for those of you who like that kind of thing, and I'll pick up some hamburgers, and hot dogs for those of us who don't."

"Sounds good to me," Rachel said, brightening. "I know the kids will love the chance to swim all day."

"I can't," Jenna said. "We're supposed to go to the beach tomorrow, with my in-laws."

"Well, if you expect us to feel sorry for you, forget it." Sara teased. "I'd take the beach over a back yard pool any day."

"Maybe so," complained Jenna. "But I'd take your company over my in-laws' any day."

After he had disposed of Missy's body, and did his best to clean up the blood, he sat in the darkened living room staring into space. After his other failures, he had been able to put them out of his mind, and return to the mundane duties of his empty life. A life that consisted of work, eating, sleeping, watching television, and feeding his dogs. He had been able to go months, sometimes more than a year, before something he saw, or heard, would start him on his mission again. But, this time it was different. He couldn't seem to let it go.

As he sat there, he kept going over the events of the night in his mind. Missy was going to get the punishment that she deserved, that she needed. He had felt so powerful. A feeling that he craved, but rarely experienced.

Now it was over, and the pain he felt was unbearable. Not the pain of Missy's death, as far as he was concerned she deserved that too, but the pain of losing that feeling of power.

He thought about Timmy, and wondered if the fact that his tormentor was gone forever, would make him happy. He even considered driving by Timmy's house, to see if he was happily learning to ride his two wheeler. Then he realized how dangerous that would be. Missy had only been missing for a few days, and the police would surely be watching her street for strangers.

Thinking about Timmy made him remember himself when he was that age. He didn't like to think about that time, and could usually push the memories away when they started to surface, but this time they washed over him like a wave. He remembered the rage that he felt whenever one of the other children would call him names or push him around, but he remembered that before he ever felt the rage he felt the pain. It was a deep, burning feeling that started in the pit of his stomach, and spread through his body. Not unlike the pain he was feeling now. Eventually, he had learned to turn the pain into anger. The anger wasn't easy to control, but it was much easier to bear.

Since he had been small for his age, and not very strong, he could never direct his anger at his tormentors. He had to keep it inside, where it grew and festered until he had finally understood why it was there, and how to use it.

After almost three years, and three failures, the pain almost made him want to give up his mission. As he sat there, he concentrated on turning the pain into anger, as he had done when he was a little boy. He first turned his anger on Missy. If the little bitch hadn't tried to get away, she would still be alive. Next he turned his anger on his dogs. If they hadn't started barking so furiously, he never would have forgotten to lock the door. Next he turned his anger on whoever those people were, running down the street. If they hadn't started the dogs barking, none of this would have happened.

For the first time, he wondered who they were, and what they had been doing. He had been so preoccupied that it never dawned on him how strange it was to see people running down the street in the middle of the night. Is that why his dogs had gone crazy? What had they been doing out there? He thought he had better go out and look around his property again, as soon as it got light.

With that decided, he turned his attention to trying to put Missy out of his mind, but this time it wasn't working. The craving for that feeling of power was already starting to grow. It's too soon, *he thought.* Too soon to try again, *he corrected himself, but maybe not too soon to start looking."*

Chapter 15

Rachel, Sara, and their families got together on Sunday, as they had planned. As usual Rachel and Sara were preparing the food, while their husbands sat inside, watching a baseball game.

"Why is it that we always have to do all the work, while those two 'Neanderthals' sit in there doing nothing?" Rachel complained.

"Good question, Scott's reasoning this time is that since this get together was my idea, I could handle it."

"Well as lame as it is, as least he gave you a reason. Michael doesn't seem to need an excuse to do nothing."

While the women were getting the food ready, Taran, Joey, Amanda and Brian were in the pool. Everyone was taking turns jumping in, to see who could make the biggest splash. Brian always made the smallest one, so he finally gave up, and climbed up on to a float. When one of Taran's jumps caused the water to splash over his head, Brian said, "Knock it off you guys, you're splashing me."

"Oh Brian, stop being such a baby." Amanda said "If you're in a swimming pool, you're going to get wet."

Ignoring Brian's complaints, Joey jumped in again, causing another wave to wash over him.

"I said stop it," Brian whined, "or I'll tell my mother."

"Why don't we get out of here," Taran said. "We can't have any fun with him around."

"Let's go ride our bikes," Joey suggested.

"Mom, can we ride our bikes?" Taran yelled over to Sara.

"All right," she yelled back. "But, don't go too far, and make sure you stay together."

"Can I go, too?" Amanda asked hopefully. The last thing she wanted was to be stuck here, alone with her brother.

"Not right now," answered Rachel. "You've been begging all week to come over here and swim, and I don't want your brother alone in the pool."

Taran and Joey decided they had better get going, before Sara changed her mind. They scrambled out of the pool, grabbed their bikes, and headed down the driveway.

"Can you believe that!" Taran exclaimed. "That kid is so annoying, and poor Amanda, it's like everything revolves around him. I feel sorry for her."

"So do I. Aren't you glad you ended up with such a great little brother like me?" Joey said, laughing.

"I don't know if I'd go that far, but I'm sure glad I didn't end up with him," Taran replied.

Amanda watched as Taran and Joey rode down the driveway. She was really looking forward to today, because she always had so much fun with them. Now because of that whining little brat, they were going off without her, and she was stuck here with him. She started to swim back and forth, ignoring her brother, and trying to hold back the tears.

"Amanda, will you push me around on the float?" Brian asked.

Amanda ignored him, and continued swimming back and forth.

"Amanda, will you push me around?" Brian asked, again.

I don't want to," she answered.

"I'll tell Mom," he threatened.

"Go ahead," she replied.

"Mom," Brian yelled. "Amanda is being mean. She won't play with me."

"He wants me to push him around like a slave," she explained, "and, I don't want to."

"Amanda, would it kill you to just push him around a couple of times?" Rachel asked. "You're not doing anything anyway."

Amanda saw the smug look of satisfaction on Brian's face, and swam over to him.

"You want me to push you? FINE!" she said, as she grabbed one end of the float, and pushed so hard that it overturned.

Brian went under the water, and came up gasping for air.

"What happened?" Rachel asked with concern, as she rushed over to the edge of the pool.

"Amanda pushed me off the float, on purpose, and I almost drowned." Brian said, as he started to cry.

Oh, stop being such a baby," Amanda scoffed. "You did not almost drown, and it was an accident."

"It was not, you were just mad because you had to play with me," Brian said.

"Well, if you weren't such a loser you'd have some friends, and I wouldn't *have* to play with you all the time."

"AMANDA!" Rachel screamed. "I HAVE HAD IT WITH THAT MOUTH OF YOURS'! WHY DO YOU ALWAYS HAVE TO ACT LIKE SUCH A MEAN LITTLE WITCH TO BRIAN? GET OUT OF THE POOL, NOW, AND DON'T SAY ANOTHER WORD."

Amanda gave Brian a disgusted look, and climbed out of the pool. Michael came out of the house, and asked "What's going on?"

"Your daughter is being her usual mean, rotten self," Rachel answered.

"Nice talk!" Michael admonished, and then said to Amanda, "Honey, why don't you come inside with me, and watch the ball game."

Amanda ran across the yard, and disappeared into the house with her father.

Rachel brought Brian up to the deck, and busied him with helping her to make the salad.

"He does that every time," she whispered to Sara. "He never bothers to find out what she did. All he cares about is having his peace and quiet back."

Sara didn't say anything. She knew how sensitive Rachel was about her kids, and any criticism of the way she handled them, but she thought Rachel had blown this one. She didn't think it was fair to Amanda to give in to Brian's every request, and to make her always have to be the one to amuse him. Brian took advantage of that, and Amanda was beginning to resent it more, and more. She would have to think of a very diplomatic way of getting that message through to Rachel, because any direct criticism of Brian would only make her more defensive.

Sara put the hamburgers and hot dogs on the grill, and then went inside to ask Scott to see if he could find the boys.

When she came outside again, she suggested to Rachel, "Maybe you should try to spend a little time alone with Amanda. She might just need to be reassured that you love her."

"I think it might be even better if Amanda spent a *lot* more time by herself" Rachel answered, angrily.

Sara knew this was not a good time to try to reason with Rachel. She would have to wait until she was in a more receptive mood.

He had not been able to sleep since Missy's "accident". He had spent all day and night on Saturday, doing things around the house to keep himself busy. Finally, early Sunday morning, he had been so exhausted that when he had gone up to his bedroom, he collapsed on the bed. He was dreaming about Missy, reliving her tumbling down the stairs, when he forced himself awake. He could hear voices coming through the open window, and wandered over to look out. He had a full view of Sara's back yard from his window, and could see that dark haired women and her friend, on the deck near the house. He saw four children in the pool, when suddenly two of them got out, and went off on their bikes.

He had never watched what went on in the yard behind his before, he had never cared, but now he needed something to take his mind off of the other night. As he watched the two remaining children in the pool, he saw the girl grab the float the boy was lying on, and overturn it. Then he watched as the dark haired women came running over to the pool. These must be her children. He didn't even know she had children. He couldn't hear what they were saying until he heard the woman scream, "AMANDA! I HAVE HAD IT WITH THAT MOUTH OF YOURS'! WHY DO YOU ALWAYS HAVE TO ACT LIKE SUCH A MEAN LITTLE WITCH TO BRIAN? GET OUT OF THE POOL, NOW, AND DON'T SAY ANOTHER WORD."

The anger in her voice surprised him. He had spent a lot of time watching children playing, and had never heard a mother scream at one of her own children like that. Then he noticed that the little boy was crying. That must be Brian. The girl went into the house with a man, probably her father, and the woman took the boy out of the pool. He was very curious about what the girl had said to make her mother so angry, and decided he would watch them for a while. He got his listening device, opened the window a few more inches, and positioned himself so that he could see, but not be seen.

A short time later, the other two boys came back, everyone came out of the house, and they all sat down to eat. The conversation while they were eating was easy to hear, but not very interesting to him. He knew it wouldn't be, because children were usually nice to each other in front of their parents. The little girl didn't talk at all, even when someone spoke to her.

"What's wrong with you?" one of the boys finally asked her.

"My mother told me not to say another word," she answered.

"Are you satisfied?" one of the men asked the dark haired woman. "Now you have her afraid to talk."

"I give up!" the woman said, as she got up, and went into the house.

The other woman followed her, and the rest of them finished eating. When they were done, one of the boys suggested they play a game of baseball. The older boys, and even Amanda were pretty good players, but Brian wasn't. He couldn't throw the ball very far, and when it was his turn to bat he missed every time.

One of the boys tried to help him, showing him how to stand, and swing the bat, but when he missed again, Amanda laughed, and taunted him with, "Give it up Brian, you couldn't hit it if it was a basketball."

Brian threw the bat down, and started to cry. When one of the boys tried to get him to try again, he shook his head, and went over to sit on the steps.

As he watched this scene, more memories of his childhood came flooding back. He tried to push them away, but he couldn't. He remembered the times in school when he was forced to play those games. Like Brian, he wasn't very good, and the other children always taunted him because of it. None of them wanted him on their team, and they laughed at him whenever he did something wrong. He never cried, like Brian was doing, but that was only because he had learned to turn the pain into anger.

He felt that anger now, as he watched Brian sitting alone, while the other children continued with their game. He watched Amanda, and felt the anger rising inside of him. She was just like the others. Even her own mother had called her a "mean little witch". It seemed to him that she was definitely the kind he was looking for, but he would have to watch her closely for a while. Just to be sure.

Chapter 16

Concern for her friend, had caused Sara to follow Rachel into the house. She knew how angry she had been, and wanted to make sure that she was all right.

"Rachel," she called out, "where are you?"

"I'm in here," Rachel answered, from the living room.

As Sara came into the room, she could see that Rachel was not all right. She not only looked angry, but she looked like she was on the verge of tears.

"What's wrong?" Sara asked.

"Michael makes me so mad!" Rachel replied. "He always acts like Amanda is an innocent baby, and I'm the cruel villain."

"There's more to it than that," Sara stated. "I know how you look when you're mad, and there's more than anger going on with you right now."

"I think you know me a little too well."

"What is it, Rachel. Talk to me."

"I guess I'm feeling guilty. Sometimes I actually hate my own daughter, Sara. It's a horrible thing to have to admit, but it's true."

"You don't really mean that."

"But I do. Do you have any idea how much easier my life would be if she wasn't around. Every argument in our house seems to be because of her. She is constantly starting fights with Brian, and it even seems that every fight Michael and I have is because of her."

"Rachel you are very upset right now, and your anger is making you think and say things you don't mean. Amanda is only a little girl. You're talking like you think she was born bad or something."

"Maybe I do. Even when she was baby, I actually believed she didn't like me. It seemed like she cried all the time, and Michael was the only one who could calm her down. As she grew into a toddler, she was 'Daddy's little girl', and I guess I resented how close they were."

"Rachel, I had no idea you felt that way. You always seemed to dote on her when she was a baby."

"The perfect mother, right? I really wanted to be, but I couldn't help the feelings I was having."

"Rachel, you were probably suffering from post-partum depression. If you had only talked about it with someone, you could have gotten some help."

As Rachel began to cry, Sara put her arms around her, and didn't say anything. When Rachel's sobs began to subside, Sara said, "It's not too late you know. You could get some family counseling to resolve some of these things."

"I couldn't!" Rachel exclaimed, "It took everything I had to admit some of these things to you. I could never talk about this with a stranger."

"What happened after Brian was born?" Sara asked.

"It was completely different with Brian. I bonded with him immediately. He was such a sweet baby, never fussy, so different from Amanda. I expected Michael to be thrilled that he had a son, but he really didn't show much interest in him when he was baby. After Brian got older, he tried to get him into the things he was interested in, mostly sports, but Brian's never been good at those things. I think he was a disappointment to Michael."

"How did Amanda react to Brian."

"She was jealous of him from the start. Michael seemed to coddle her all the more because of it, and I guess I over compensated by spoiling Brian. We really have a screwed up family dynamics don't we? I know I wasn't fair to Amanda when she was a baby," Rachel continued, "and maybe the way she turned out is my fault, but now I have to protect Brian. His sister hates him, his father ignores him, and I'm all he has."

"Now don't get defensive, Rachel, but I think Brian knows you feel that way, and sometimes he takes advantage of that."

"Oh, I don't think so. I know Brian tends to complain to me about everything, but when I try to mediate, Amanda always manages to say the meanest, cruelest thing she can think of to hurt him. Brian cries, I get angry and punish her, and then she resents him more than ever. It's a vicious cycle, and I don't know how to stop it."

"You know, you may not be helping Brian by trying to fight all of his battles for him. He depends on you so much to solve all of his problems, that he doesn't know how to deal with them himself. When Amanda and Brian get into an argument, why don't you let them try to work it out themselves? When you always make Amanda the villain, and Brian the victim, they'll play those roles to the hilt."

"I see what you mean," Rachel said. "Sort of a self fulfilling prophecy. If I treat Brian like a victim, he'll feel like one, and never stand up for himself. And if I treat Amanda like a villain, she'll try her best to be one."

"Right, and you're the only one that can change that."

"After all this time, though, I don't know if I can just let Brian fend for himself. He always seems so vulnerable."

At that moment, Brian came into the room. He complained that he had nothing to do, because the other kids were playing baseball, and they wouldn't play anything else.

"Why don't you play with them," Sara suggested.

"I can't, I stink! When I couldn't hit the ball, Amanda laughed at me, and told me to give up," Brian answered, as he started to cry.

"See what I mean?" Rachel said to Sara, as she gathered Brian into her arms.

As Rachel put her arms around Brian, Sara noticed that his tears stopped immediately. She also noticed a peculiar look of satisfaction on his face. She wondered if this was a pattern with them, but knew that this was not the time to bring it up.

Chapter 17

He continued to watch the children playing baseball. Eventually, even the fathers joined their game, but Brian still sat on the steps watching them play. The others didn't pay any attention to him, and acted as though he wasn't even there. How could his own father ignore him like that?, the man wondered. Couldn't he see how sad he was? Didn't he even care? As he watched, Brian finally got up, and went into the house.

He wondered why the women had not come out again. They had been in there a long time. For some reason, thinking about the women made him remember the three figures he had seen running down the street the night of Missy's accident. He remembered that he was going to look around outside, as soon as it was light. Being outside in the daylight made him feel exposed, and vulnerable, but he needed the daylight if he was going to be able to see anything.

Reluctantly, he left his position at the window, went downstairs, and out the back door. He could hear the sound of the baseball game, and Amanda's laughter. He was already beginning to hate that sound.

He walked around the side of his house, and went down to the bushes that grew along the street. He noticed some of the branches in the front were broken, and there were a lot of footprints in the soft dirt. Small footprints. Either children, or women must have made them. If they were made the other night, it couldn't have been children, because he didn't think children would have been wandering around in the middle of the night. The thought that someone might have been here made him very nervous. He could picture them crouching behind the bushes, watching his house.

He walked slowly back toward the house, examining the ground as he went. He didn't see any more footprints, but the dirt here was packed harder than it was around the bushes. As he walked around the side of the house something colorful caught his eye.

Lying next to the house, almost at the corner, was a piece of material. He went over and picked it up. It was a red and yellow bow, attached to a metal clip. The kind women and girls wore in their hair. It looked familiar. He was sure he had seen it before. At first he thought maybe it had belonged to Missy, but he couldn't understand how it could have gotten out here. Besides, he knew Missy hadn't been wearing anything like that. He was sure he would have remembered. He stood there for a few minutes, trying to remember where he might have seen it before. Then he noticed something close to the edge of the house, where the dirt was softer. Another footprint. Small, like the ones around the bushes. Someone had been here, he thought with alarm. Someone had been right here, almost in his back yard. Was that why his dogs had gone crazy the other night? This was bad, very bad. He had always felt safe here, it was the only place he did feel safe, and now someone had invaded his privacy. He had to do something about this. But what? Then he remembered the warehouse where he worked. They had lights there, that would automatically go on if anyone were sneaking around outside. That's what he would do. It might not stop anyone from sneaking around, but it would sure let him know if they did.

He waited until dark, and then drove to the big building supply place, in the next town. The clerk knew just what he was looking for. They had several types of lights, and since he didn't know anything about electrical wiring, he chose the kind that were battery operated. The clerk told him that the batteries were good for 10 hours of continuous operation, but he bought extra batteries anyway.

As soon as he got home, he installed a light at each corner of his house. He adjusted the sensors over and over, until he was sure the lights would only turn on if someone got very close to the house. He took the bulb out of the light at the back corner that he always drove by when he parked his van. He didn't want a light coming on every time he came home. He would only put the bulb in when it was necessary. When he was there, or had to be sure that no one came near the house.

He went back into the house, and up to his bedroom. He looked out the window, and was disappointed that Sara's yard was dark, and empty. He sat staring out of the window, wondering how he was going to be able to watch Amanda. He would have to find out where she lived, but he would have to be extra careful. Her mother made him very nervous.

The more he thought about Rachel, the more nervous he became. He had never paid any attention to the children that lived around him. He had always looked for the "right type" far away from his own hometown, even traveling to nearby states. He knew from watching TV movies, that when a child was missing, the police always looked to the family first, and friends or neighbors second. That's why he made sure his search never took him too close to home. The more he thought about it, the surer he became that selecting someone so close to home would be a mistake.

Although he was sure Amanda was the type he was looking for, he thought maybe he had better look elsewhere. He could feel the excitement of another search growing within him, and the bitter disappointment of what had happened with Missy, fading away. He was sure Timmy would be all right, now that his tormentor was gone. Although he tried not to think about her, his thoughts kept returning to Amanda, and how Brian needed protection from her. Brian was so small and defenseless, just like he had been when he was a little boy. He needed someone to look out for him, someone to make the cruelty stop. With a visible shake, he forced his thoughts away from her.

When his mission had first become clear to him, he was so sure that he was supposed to make the cruel children realize what they were, and change. He was sure that once that happened, they would become good, and treat all the other children with kindness. Now he wasn't so sure that was possible. Maybe cruel children can't change. Maybe that wasn't his purpose at all. Maybe his purpose all along was not to change them, but to eliminate them. If that were true, then he hadn't failed three times. He had succeeded, because they were supposed to die. But, even if they were supposed to die, they were also supposed to suffer. The way they had caused others to suffer. The way they had caused him to suffer.

Chapter 18

Amanda was lying on her bed, in the dark. Her mother hadn't spoken to her since the incident in the pool, and no one else had mentioned it either. Her father had tried to make her feel better, but she could still feel the sting of her mother's words. She had called her a 'mean little witch', and Amanda had never heard her sound so angry. When they had come home, Amanda had felt too uncomfortable to be around her mother, and had gone straight to her room. Lying there she thought about everything that had happened. She liked being at Aunt Sara's because, even when her mother got mad at her, Aunt Sara never acted like she didn't like her. She even looked like she felt bad for her. She liked being with Taran and Joey too. Even though they were older than she was, they were so much fun to play with. She wished that *they* were her brothers, instead of *Brian*.

Brian was no fun to play with at all. He was such a baby, and he always cried whenever he didn't get his way. He would cry to their mother, and then she would make Amanda do whatever he wanted to do, or blame her because he was crying. It made Amanda so mad that she always ended up saying something bad to him. She didn't really mean the terrible things she said, but he always made her so mad. She even felt bad after, but it was too late to take them back.

She wondered why her mother always took Brian's side against her. She knew that some of the things she said *were* really mean, but her mother seemed to take Brian's side before Amanda even said anything. Like today, not only couldn't she go riding with Taran and Joey, but her mother was going to make her push Brian around the pool, like he was a king and she was his slave. All he had to do was complain in that whiny little voice, and he got what ever he wanted.

If her mother thought the things she said to Brian were so awful, how come she didn't think the things her mother said to her were just as bad? She had always been sure that her mother loved Brian more than she loved her. Now she was sure that her mother didn't love her at all, and she knew that it was all Brian's fault.

Amanda heard the door to her room opening, so she closed her eyes, and pretended that she was asleep. She knew it was her mother, checking to see if she was awake.

She was probably going to yell at her some more. When she heard the door close again, she turned over, and began to cry. She let the tears flow silently from her eyes. This was the only time she would let herself cry, when no one could see her. She would never let anyone see her cry.

After Rachel had admitted her feelings to Sara, she had felt ashamed. She didn't feel as though Sara had been judging her, but she had never admitted those feelings even to herself, and when she had said them out loud she realized how terrible they sounded. Had she actually said that she didn't love her own daughter? That she didn't even like her? She didn't really feel that way, she couldn't. Amanda was her daughter. She loved her. Maybe she didn't like some of the things she said, and did, but she loved her.

Rachel always felt terrible after these episodes with Amanda. She always regretted the things she had said to her. She knew she should apologize, and tell Amanda she didn't mean them, but the anger she felt was so intense that she couldn't.

Sara had told her that she was the only one that could change things, and maybe she should start now. Amanda had gone to her room as soon as they had gotten home, but Rachel didn't think she was sleeping. She would go in, and talk to her right now. She would tell her that she loved her, and apologize for the things she had said today. She went to Amanda's room, quietly opened the door, and looked in. The room was dark, and Amanda was asleep. She didn't want to wake her up, so she decided to wait until the morning.

The next morning, everyone overslept. Michael was late for work, and the kids would probably be late for school. The place was a madhouse, as everyone rushed around trying to get ready at the same time. With all of the confusion, there was no time to talk to Amanda that morning, so Rachel resolved to do it as soon as she got home from school.

Amanda was glad that they were in such a rush that morning. She didn't want to have to face her mother's silent treatment. She knew her mother would be so sweet to Brian, and only talk to her if she had to. She had taken her time getting dressed, so that she wouldn't even have time for breakfast, and would have to rush out the door. She was especially glad that she had play rehearsal after school, because her father would be home by the time she got there. Amanda had cried herself to sleep, the night before, but when she woke up that morning she didn't feel like crying, she was just mad. Mad at her mother, and mad at Brian.

Soon after Amanda and Brian had left, Rachel remembered that Amanda would not be home right after school. The fourth grade was putting on a play for the Memorial Day program, and they had rehearsals after school on Mondays and Wednesdays. She knew the longer she waited, the less likely she was to talk to her daughter. The guilt and shame she had felt last night was fading, and the familiar feelings of irritation with Amanda, and sympathy for Brian, were returning.

She also felt slightly annoyed at Sara. She loved her like a sister, but sometimes she could be so damn logical. She could look at the cold hard facts, and know exactly what should be done, but she didn't have to live with it. She didn't have a seven-year-old son, who was ignored by his father, hated by his sister, and depended on her to protect him. Brian was so innocent, and he didn't deserve to have to suffer Amanda's cruel ridicule every day.

The more she thought about it, the more annoyed she became. She wished that she had never admitted those things to Sara. She was afraid that Sara would not let it go, and try to make her face those feelings. "Why can't I learn when to keep my mouth shut?" Rachel wondered aloud.

Chapter 19

When he awoke on Monday morning, he thought about going back to the park where he had first seen Missy. It was just the kind of place he preferred. There were a lot of trees, and it was crowded enough so that he wouldn't be noticed, but he knew he could not go back there. He never went to the same place twice, because that increased the chance that he would be remembered. He took out the large book he had purchased for just this purpose. It listed parks and recreation areas all over New England. He decided on Massachusetts this time. He had never chosen his own state before, but maybe that had been a mistake. After all, excluding one particular state might be just as conspicuous as limiting himself to one. He was very proud of himself, for even thinking of that. "I'm getting really good at this." he thought.

He looked for parks and playgrounds that were at least an hour away. He rejected ones that were in towns that were so small that a stranger would be noticed immediately. He finally found what he was looking for, a park that had a duck pond, hiking trails, and a playground. He decided to go there on Saturday, when it would probably be crowded.

He was anxious to get going, as soon as he came home from work on Saturday, but he knew that 7:30 in the morning was too early. He wanted to arrive there in the early afternoon, when he knew the park would be the most crowded. He made himself something to eat, and tried to get some sleep. He always had trouble sleeping once he had decided to begin his search. The combination of the excitement and anxiety he felt were almost unbearable. As he tried to sleep his thoughts kept returning to Amanda, and he forcibly pushed them away. He had to stop thinking about her. She was out of his reach, and he had to concentrate on the ones that were not. Maybe once he found someone else he would be able to do that. He had to.

He tossed and turned, and tried to sleep, until finally it was almost time for him to leave. He put new batteries into the listening device. He prepared a chloroform soaked rag, and placed it in an airtight container. He didn't think he would need that today, he never had on the first day of his search, but he wanted to be prepared. He took the directions he had copied from his book, and started off.

When he arrived at his destination, he was pleased. It was a large park with many people, and many children. There was a long narrow parking area along the edge of the road.

He pulled into a parking space facing the park, and sat there for a while, surveying the scene. There was a playground at one end, and a baseball field at the other. In the middle was a small building that had some kind of snack bar on one side, and public restrooms on the other. Trees stretched out across the back, with a wooden archway in the middle. He assumed that the hiking trails and duck pond were back there. There were benches scattered around the perimeter of the playground, and one set of bleachers behind the outfield fence at the baseball field. Although the ball field was empty, he knew it must be a little league field, because it was so small.

He positioned the earpiece in his ear, and slipped the listening device into his shirt pocket, but didn't turn it on. He got out of his van, grabbed the paperback book on the seat, and headed for the playground. As he sat on one of the benches, pretending to read, he watched the children playing. He sat there for over an hour, watching the children come and go, waiting for the right one. He was disappointed that there didn't seem to be anyone that interested him. While some of the children argued over whose turn it was on the swings, no one seemed to be especially cruel to anyone else.

He started to feel hungry and thirsty, and noticed that the snack bar had opened for business. He walked over, ordered a hot dog and soda, and stood looking around. He noticed, for the first time, that there were children on the ball field in uniforms. He was right, it was a little league field. The boys looked to be about nine or ten years old. He knew the game hadn't started yet, because the boys were paired up on the field tossing baseballs back and forth.

When he got his food, he glanced over towards the playground. The same children were there, and nothing of interest appeared to be happening, so he wandered over to the baseball field. He stood near the outfield fence, and watched the boys warming up. One slightly over weight boy caught his attention. He missed the ball more often than he caught it, and then he would run slowly and clumsily to retrieve it. He decided to sit on the bleachers for a while, and watch.

The boy that was paired up with the one that had caught his eye yelled, "Frankie, can't you even try to catch the stupid thing?"

"I am trying, Bobby," Frankie said. "Can't you throw it a little easier?"

"Sure," Bobby answered. "How's this?"

Bobby threw the ball as hard as he could. Frankie ducked, as the ball went whizzing by his head, and landed at the other end of the field.

"Are you trying to kill me?" Frankie asked, in shock.

"Oh stop being such a baby, and go get the ball." Bobby said.

As Frankie lumbered after the ball, Bobby said to the boy next to him, "Look at that. It's not bad enough that he can't catch, he can't even run. Even if he could hit the ball into the outfield, he wouldn't even make it to first base before they tagged him."

"Bobby, if he hadn't ducked, you really could have hurt him. Why don't you give him a break?" the other boy responded.

"Why doesn't he give us a break, and get off our team. It's a miracle that we ever win a game with him around."

Before Frankie got back with the ball, the coach called the team into the dugout.

He watched the team hurry off the field, and his eyes burned with fury. He wanted to watch the baseball game, and Bobby, but he wasn't sure if he should. Would the parents of these boys notice a stranger, and wonder who he was?

As the people began arriving for the game, he noticed that most of them carried lawn chairs, and sat along the first or third baselines, depending on which dugout their son's team was using. Others, but not as many, sat on the bleachers where he was sitting. Some of them knew each other, and exchanged hellos, but most of them seemed uninterested in the people around them. No one looked at him as if he didn't belong there, and he began to feel safer.

It looked as if it wasn't unusual around here for people to simply stop by the field to watch a game, even if their own son's weren't playing. He decided to stay, and see what happened. He had been able to hear the boys clearly when they were warming up, because they had been close to the outfield fence, but now they were much further away. He reached into his pocket, and turned on the listening device. He wanted to be able to hear every word that Bobby said.

When the game started, Frankie's team was at bat. The first boy struck out, and the next two got on base. Bobby was up to bat next, and as he had expected the boy hit the ball and drove in two runs.

He was disappointed when Frankie didn't get up to bat during that inning, and was also disappointed when Frankie stayed in the dugout, as his team took the field. He wasn't surprised to see Bobby saunter up to the pitcher's mound, and begin throwing some warm-up pitches. By the fifth inning, he knew that Bobby was the star of the team, and Frankie had no talent at all.

Frankie struck out his first two turn's at bat. The third time he actually hit the ball, but was put out easily at first base. Each time he came up to bat, Bobby made a belittling comment like, "Well

76

here's an automatic out." or "Let him hit you Frankie, that's the only way you'll get on base." Every time Bobby made one of his comments, the coach would reprimand him. He told him he was supposed to encourage his teammates, but that didn't stop Bobby.

The man realized, from the conversation around him, that little league rules required the coaches to use each player in at least three innings when the team was in the field. Since the games lasted six innings, Frankie spent three innings in the dugout, and three innings in right field. Once when a fly ball was hit in his direction, Frankie covered his head, and the ball dropped ten feet in front of him. He lumbered after the ball, and threw it toward first base, as the batter rounded second and headed for third. What turned out to be the winning run was scored, and standing on the pitcher's mound, Bobby yelled, "Frankie, how can you be so stupid? You not only missed an easy fly ball, but you don't even know what to do with the ball when you get it. You're such a loser." Frankie put his head down, and turned away from Bobby. Although he couldn't see his face, he knew there were probably tears in his eyes. He stared at Bobby, and felt the anger in him begin to grow.

After the game, he waited in his van until he saw Bobby come into the parking lot with another man, he assumed was his father. When they got into their car and drove off, he followed them to find out where they lived. It was not far from the park, but he was disappointed to find that it was a quiet dead end street. He would not be able to drive by Bobby's house, and watch for him as he had done with Missy. Someone would surely notice a strange vehicle on the street.

He decided he would go back to the park every day. Since it was so close to his house, maybe Bobby spent a lot of time there. Although he thought Bobby was the kind he was looking for, he would have to watch him closely for a while, just to be sure.

Chapter 20

For the first time that she could remember, Sara was not looking forward to going over to Rachel's for coffee. She had known Rachel for years, but she realized yesterday how little she really knew about her. Although she had tried not to show it, the things Rachel had said about Amanda had shocked her. She wondered again if she had really meant what she had said, or if it was just the anger and frustration talking. She wanted to talk to her about it, but she knew Rachel well enough to know that she would become very defensive, and resent any indication that she was not 'the perfect mother'. Brian had shown yesterday how manipulative he could be, but Rachel had such a blind spot when it came to him, she would never believe that.

Sara sighed, and got ready to walk over to Rachel's. She wondered how they had become such good friends when they were so different. Sara hated confrontation, and Rachel seemed to thrive on it. She was strong and opinionated, and at times tended to dominate Sara. Sara hated the fact that she allowed that to happen, but Rachel's friendship meant a lot to her, and she didn't want to do anything to jeopardize it. She was about ready to put the whole episode out of her mind, when the hurt look on Amanda's face, and the satisfied look on Brian's came back to her. Maybe she would have to chance the confrontation. She would have to see what kind of a mood Rachel was in this morning before she decided anything.

Rachel tensed when she saw Sara walking up the driveway. She hoped that they could have a pleasant visit this morning. She wasn't in the mood for any conflicts. She put on a bright smile, opened the door, and said, "Hi Sara, I hope we didn't leave you with too much of a mess last night."

"No more of a mess than we leave you with. How are you doing this morning?"

"Well, we all overslept so it was a mad house here for a while. I'm just starting to calm down."

"Rachel, is there anything you want to talk about?"

Sara saw Rachel tense up, and feeling her courage evaporate, immediately wished she had kept her mouth shut. Rachel was about to say something, when Christie appeared at the back door. Sara saw this as the perfect opportunity to backtrack, and said, "I mean about that house on Rocky Ridge. If you still think there's something going on there, we can figure out what to do."

Rachel relaxed, and decided to try to get Christie going. She winked at Sara, and said, "Well I'll tell you, after what I saw Friday night, I think we had better do something, and fast."

"What did you see?" Christie asked warily.

"Oh that's right. You weren't there when we got back, and I didn't see you all weekend," Rachel answered. "Well I went right up to that house, and looked in the window."

"You didn't!" Christie cried.

"Sure I did, and do you know what I saw?"

"I don't think I want to know."

Sara had been trying to hold it in, but she couldn't control it any longer. She burst out laughing, and Rachel joined her. Christie looked from one to other trying to figure out what was so funny. Suddenly she realized that Rachel had been teasing her, and said, "I'm glad you two think that was funny. You almost scared me to death."

"Well it serves you right for running out on us," Rachel countered. "What if something did happen to us? You were the only one who knew where we went."

"Didn't you get my note? Danny was having a problem with Jimmy, and I had to go home."

Rachel was tempted to ask Christie how Danny had called her, when her number didn't show up on Sara's caller ID, but her mood had improved considerably within the past few minutes, and she didn't want to get into anything that would ruin that.

"Okay, we'll forgive you this time," she said.

"Well, what did happen when you went over there?" Christie asked.

"Nothing," Rachel answered, as she looked over at Sara. "We just went for a walk."

"I thought you were going to check out that house," Christie said.

"God, Christie you must think I'm totally insane. I was just kidding around. Did you really think I was serious?"

"Of course not," Christie answered, defensively. "I was kidding too."

"Rachel, is there anything in this morning's paper about that little girl that was missing?" Sara asked, changing the subject. "Did they find her yet?"

"I don't know," Rachel answered. "I haven't even looked at the paper."

When Rachel opened the paper they saw a picture of a little girl on the front page. She looked to be about nine or ten years old. She was pretty with long, light colored hair, and a beautiful smile. The headline read:

Missy Harper Still Missing

Rachel scanned the story and said, "They don't seem to have any leads at all. At least none that they're letting out. They're asking for anyone who may have seen something the day she disappeared to contact the police."

"Where does she live?" Sara asked.

"Wilmington, Connecticut. It's in the southwestern part of the state."

"Does it say anything about the other two that they mentioned last week?"

"It says that they're still looking for a connection. So far they haven't found one, and since they were all from different states, and the timing is so far apart, they don't think they're related."

"I think they are," Sara announced. "Look at that guy who killed that 12 year old boy from

Massachusetts. A few years later he kidnapped, and killed, a 12-year-old girl from New York. If he hadn't confessed to both of them, they never would have thought they were related either."

"Maybe they do think they're related, but they're just saying that to throw this guy off the track," Christie suggested.

"And let him feel really secure, so he can do it again and again. That would be really smart." Rachel answered, sarcastically.

"I hope they find her," Sara said, as she stared at Missy's picture. "She's such a beautiful little girl. Her family must be devastated."

Chapter 21

He went back to the park the very next day. He expected to see Bobby and Frankie playing another baseball game, and was disappointed when there were two different teams on the field. He knew nothing about little league games, and didn't understand why they weren't playing again. He walked over to the playground, and sat on one of the benches. He watched the different children playing there, but was not really interested in any of them. Once he had made a selection, that was the only thing he thought about. He wasn't really sure yet if Bobby was the right one, and he had to see him more, watch him more, to be sure.

He stayed at the park for the next few hours, watching the arrival of each new child, and feeling disappointed when it wasn't him. He finally gave up, and decided to go home. He went by Bobby's street on the way home, and looked down the street as he drove past. He saw some children playing street hockey, and was tempted to find out if Bobby was one of them, but he knew that would be a mistake. He had to be patient. If he took too many chances, he would fail.

He went back to the park every day for the next week. He was sure Bobby would show up there eventually, and he wanted to be there when he did. He timed himself so he would arrive there after 3:00 PM during the week, because he knew the children would not be there before then. He was nervous about someone noticing, and remembering him, so he took great pains to change his appearance. One day he wore a baseball cap pulled low over his face. Another day he wore a short blond wig, and another day he wore a long brown one, pulled back in a ponytail. Sometimes, he even wore different layers of clothes, so that he looked like he was heavier one day than the next.

His patience paid off on Saturday morning. He arrived at the park at 10:00 AM, and saw four or five boys setting up makeshift ramps in the grassy area near the playground. His excitement began to grow, when he saw that Bobby was one of them. He was disappointed that Frankie wasn't there, but at least Bobby was. He got out of his van, and headed for one of the benches. He had the paperback book in his hand, but he didn't even pretend to read it. He couldn't take his eyes off of Bobby.

When the boys had finished setting up the ramps, they all ran over to where their bikes were laying on the ground, and picked them up. Bobby yelled,
"I'm first."
He rode toward the ramps picking up speed as he went. When he went up the first ramp, he became airborne for a few seconds. He landed on the back tire, and immediately straightened out. They had the ramps spaced far enough apart so that Bobby had time to pick up enough speed, before he reached the second one to repeat what he had done with the first. He did the same with the third ramp, and then came skidding to a stop next to the other boys.
"That was awesome!" he said.
"My turn next," one of the other boys shouted, as he took off on his bike.
For the next hour, the boys took turns jumping the ramps. He could see that Bobby was by far the best rider in the group, and for some reason he couldn't understand, that angered him. He kept hoping that he would fall, and although some of the other boys did, Bobby continued to keep his balance, landing smoothly every time. Was this boy the best at everything he did?, he thought.

It seemed so unfair to him that someone like this boy excelled at everything he did, and someone like Frankie, or Brian, or he himself, failed at everything they tried. Bobby and his friends continued their riding, and just as he was deciding that maybe Bobby wasn't exactly the type he was looking for, Frankie rode up on his bike.

The man noticed that the bikes the other boys were riding were small, and lightweight, while Frankie's bike was bigger, heavier, and had much larger wheels. Frankie stood, and watched the other boys for a few minutes, and then he said, "Hey that looks like fun. Can I try it?"

"Are you nuts? This is a BMX track. You would never make it on that piece of junk you're riding," Bobby answered.

"This is not a piece of junk!" Frankie complained. "It's a mountain bike."

"So go ride up a mountain," Bobby responded "Only BMX riders are allowed here."

"Oh let him try the jumps, Bobby," one of the other boys said. "He can't hurt them."

"Yeah, let him try it," the other boys joined in.

"I guess I'm out voted, so go ahead," Bobby responded. "It's your funeral."

Frankie looked at Bobby cautiously. It seemed as though he was not sure what to do. Finally, he got on his bike, and headed towards the first ramp. He went up the ramp, and cleared the end of it by a few inches. He came down hard, but kept his balance, and headed for the next one. He didn't gain very much speed before he went up the next ramp. When he came down, his back wheel caught the edge of the wood. Frankie flew over the handlebars, and his bike flipped over landing on top of him.

The other boys ran over to see if he was all right, all except Bobby. When Frankie got up, the man could see the side of his face was scraped and bruised.

"You ride a bike like you play baseball," Bobby taunted.

"Shut up!" Frankie yelled, as he gingerly touched the side of his face.

The man silently rooted for Frankie, thinking, You tell him, Frankie. You make him shut up.

"You shut up," Bobby responded. "We lost our game last week because of you. Every game we lose is because of you. Why don't you go home, and play with *your sister's dolls? You're too fat, clumsy, and stupid to do anything else."*

"Frankie, you really better go home, that cut on your face is starting to bleed," one of the other boys said.

Frankie picked up his bike, and started to walk out of the park. He tried to hold back the tears, but the man could see them slowing rolling down his cheeks.

"Why do you always have to pick on him like that?" one of the boys asked Bobby. "He really got hurt, you know."

"He's a wimp, and a cry baby," Bobby answered, with disgust. "I hope I never see him again."

The man's eyes burned with fury, as he looked at Bobby. Be careful what you wish for, he thought.

Chapter 22

After Sara had gone home, Rachel half listened to Christie's chatter, as she thought about the past few days. She was grateful that Sara hadn't mentioned their conversation about Amanda. Maybe, she had been wrong. Maybe, Sara wasn't going to make an issue of it. She hoped she wouldn't, but she decided that she would try to get along better with Amanda. She also would be very careful of how she talked to her daughter around Sara. Rachel didn't want to give Sara any excuse to bring up what she had confessed to her.

Rachel also began to think about the house on Rocky Ridge. How could she have been so foolish to try to get closer without any kind of a plan. She had been so scared that night that she had wanted to convince herself that all of her feelings were just her imagination, but it hadn't worked. She was glad that Sara had gone along with the story that she had told Christie. She knew from what had happened on Friday night that she couldn't depend on Christie, so she wasn't going to confide in her anymore either. She still felt that something was wrong in that house, but she wasn't going to take any more foolish chances. She would have to talk to Sara when they were alone. Maybe she would have some ideas about what to do.

Amanda went about her normal activities at school, but her mind kept returning to her mother. She didn't like the way she was feeling, but she couldn't help it. The intensity of the anger she felt scared her, and she wanted it to go away. She tried to think of the good things about her mother. The way she would buy her favorite snacks at the grocery store, when she asked her to. The way she would always agree to drive her to her friends house, or let them have sleepovers.

Actually, she realized, the only time they really had problems was when Brian was around. Amanda knew the things she said to her brother were not very nice, but he made her so mad. All he had to do was cry, and their mother felt sorry for him. She knew that the things she said to Brian only made it worse, but she couldn't seem to stop herself. She decided that she would try harder than ever to be nice to Brian from now on, at least when their mother was around.

As Sara walked home, she thought about Rachel, and the events of the past few days. She hated the fact that she was such a marshmallow when it came to Rachel. Did she really think they wouldn't be friends anymore if she didn't agree with her about everything? Did she want to take the chance? Maybe she was making too much of what Rachel had said about Amanda. Rachel had been upset, and she had probably said a lot of things she didn't really mean.

For the first time since they had moved to Eden Park, Sara was glad Christie had come over. She had given her the idea to change the direction in which her conversation was headed, and talk about the house on Rocky Ridge instead. She was puzzled about why Rachel had not told Christie what had really happened on Friday night. Rachel either didn't want to talk about it in front of Christie, or she didn't want to talk about it at all.

When Sara got to the house on Rocky Ridge, she felt the hair rise on the back of her neck. It felt like someone was watching her, and she looked at windows as she went by. The drapes were drawn back, but the house still looked deserted. It is a strange house. What kind of a person would live there? she thought. Am I getting as bad as Rachel, or am I just starting to understand the feelings she has been having? She felt a chill go down her back, and started to walk faster. Maybe there is something wrong with that house, she thought, and maybe we *should* find out what it is.

As soon as she got home, she called Rachel.
"Can you come over, when you get a chance?" she asked. "I have to talk to you."
"What's wrong Sara?" Rachel asked. "You sound so strange."

"I just really need to talk to you, and I'd like to do it without Christie around."

"I'll be over as soon as I can," Rachel said.

Chapter 23

He watched Frankie leave, and sat there as the boys continued to ride their bikes. He knew now that Bobby was the type he was looking for, and what he had to do. But, he knew that he couldn't do anything about it here. It was much too public, and there was a chance that someone would remember him. He had to be able to get to Bobby when he was alone, and that was not going to be easy. He couldn't wait near his house, as he had done with Missy.

He noticed the boys leaving one by one, saying they had to go home for one reason or another. Bobby told them that he didn't have to be home until one o'clock, for lunch. The man glanced at his watch, and saw that it was already 12:30. He decided he had to follow Bobby, when he left the park. He knew where he lived, and that he would have to go through the parking lot on his way home, so he went to his van, and waited.

At 12:45, Bobby came riding past him. He pulled out of the parking lot in time to see the boy turn the corner, onto a side street. As he followed him, he began to realize that there would be plenty of opportunities to catch him alone. The street that he was on now had woods on both sides, and very few houses. He had expected to see the boy go to the end of the street, and was surprised when about halfway down, he turned into the woods. As he drove slowly by the spot where he had seen Bobby go into the woods, he noticed a path. When he got to the end of the street he was on, he turned in the direction Bobby had gone, and realized that Bobby lived on the next street. He stopped at the corner, and sat there for a few minutes. Suddenly, he saw him come out of the woods, directly across from his house. That must be a shortcut, he thought. He probably always goes that way when he goes home. A plan began to form in his mind. As long as Bobby was at the park next week, it should work.

During the following week, he found it hard to concentrate on anything else. He made sure his

special room was ready, and that he had all the
supplies he needed. As Saturday approached, he became
more and more anxious. He always felt this way once
he had decided on a day, and he relished the feeling.
Most of the time, he felt empty inside, so even
anxiety was a welcome change.

Saturday morning finally arrived, and he drove to
an animal shelter. He was careful to choose a place
that he had never been to before, and he picked out
the smallest puppy they had. With his supplies safely
stored in the back of the van, he drove to the park.
He was happy to see Bobby there, as he had been the
previous week, riding his bike with the other boys.
He was not surprised to see that Frankie was not
there.

Since it was only 11:30, he knew he had some time
to kill, and drove to a diner a short distance away.
He ordered some food, took it outside, and sat in the
parking lot while he ate. At 12:30, he drove to the
street where he had seen Bobby go into the woods. He
parked his van where he knew Bobby would have to ride
past him, got out of the van, opened the door in the
back, and waited.

He hadn't been waiting long, when he saw Bobby
coming down the street. As he had hoped, he was
alone. When Bobby was almost up to him, he took the
puppy out of the van. As Bobby came closer, he said,
"Excuse me, do you know of anyone who may have lost a
dog? I found this puppy on the side of the road, and
I'm trying to find it's owner."

Bobby stopped a few feet away from him, and asked
"What does it look like?"

He held the puppy in his arms, as he had done
before, so that only the tip of it's snout was
visible.

"He so squirmy, that if I don't hold on tight, I'll
drop him," he said. "Why don't you come over, and
take a look?"

Bobby looked at him suspiciously, and said, "I
don't think so. I'm allergic to dogs, and I don't
know anyone who lost one anyway."

Before the man could answer or react, Bobby sped off, and disappeared into the woods.

He stood there looking down at the animal in his arms. He felt confused, and didn't know what to do. He was so sure that it would work. It had always worked before. He felt rage begin to boil up inside of him, until he thought he would scream. Suddenly, he threw the puppy down on the side of the road, climbed into his van, and drove off.

By the time he got home, he was much calmer, and the rage he had felt earlier had been replaced by a deep feeling of despair. He knew that it was important for him to control his temper, but it was getting much harder for him to do that. The puppy hadn't worked. He thought about the puppy now, and felt badly about how he had treated it. He hoped that someone would find it. He decided that maybe it was a good thing that he had left the puppy there. If Bobby had told anyone about their meeting, it would be less suspicious if someone in the neighborhood actually found the stray dog.

He knew that he had to give up his plan on taking Bobby. Even if he did think of something else, now that he had spoken to the boy he would never be able to take the chance of approaching him again. As he sat there, he remembered the look on Frankie's face, and the silent tears that had rolled down his cheeks. He couldn't give up! Frankie needed him to stop the torment this cruel child inflicted on him. He had to find a way.

He thought about the woods near Bobby's house. He remembered how, when he was a boy, he could hide in his own woods without being seen. Another plan began to form in his mind. He would go back tonight, after dark, and explore the woods near the boy's house. If the woods were the way he had pictured them, and he was very careful, it might just work.

Chapter 24

Rachel was impatient for Christie to leave. She had never heard Sara sound so nervous before, and she wanted to find out what it was all about. When it looked as if Christie had decided to settle in for the morning, Rachel said, "I hate to rush you out, but I really have to go grocery shopping this morning. I don't have a thing for dinner tonight."

"I have plenty of stuff in my freezer if you need something," Christie offered.

"Thanks anyway, but there are a lot of things I need"

Reluctantly, Christie gathered up her son, who was watching cartoons in the next room, and headed out the door. As soon as she was gone, Rachel got into her car, and drove over to Sara's. At least it would look like she was going shopping.

When she got to Sara's house, she found her sitting on the deck, drinking a glass of wine. She had never seen Sara drink anything stronger than coffee, while it was still daylight. As Rachel came out on the deck, Sara looked up, and said, "I feel so stupid, I think I let my imagination run wild."

"About what?" Rachel asked, cautiously. She was afraid Sara was going to talk about Amanda.

"About that stupid house on Rocky Ridge," Sara answered.

"Why, what happened?"

"Well, when I walked by that house on the way home this morning, I got a strange feeling like someone was watching me. I looked at the windows, and didn't see anyone, but I got the feeling something was wrong. Oh, I can't explain it. It's stupid. *I* feel stupid."

Rachel should have felt relieved, but she didn't. She had tried to put the house out of her mind. She had tried to convince herself that she had let *her* imagination get away from her. Now solid, logical Sara was getting the same feelings that she had. There had to be something to it. It couldn't be in both of their minds.

"You're not stupid Sara, and you know it. I have a pretty wild imagination sometimes, but you are the most down to earth person that I know. If you have a feeling about that house, then there is probably a reason for it."

"I don't know what it is." Sara said, thoughtfully "I've been sitting here, and trying to figure it out. I just have a bad feeling, and I don't know why."

"You don't have to convince me. I know exactly what you mean. There's nothing specific I can put my finger on either, but I get such a creepy feeling whenever I see that place."

"Damn you Rachel! I was perfectly happy in my new home, and now you have me feeling like I have Dr. Frankenstein, or someone equally ghoulish, as a neighbor."

"Sara, I've talked about that house for weeks, and you and Christie just laughed it off. You know I'm not the reason you started feeling this way."

"Hey, speaking of Christie, why didn't you want to tell her what really happened Friday night?"

"I guess it's because of the way she bailed out on us. It makes me feel like I can't trust her. The last thing I need is her running around the neighborhood, telling everyone that I'm some kind of a nut, who tries to look in people's windows."

"I know what you mean. That's why I wanted you to come over here today. I wanted to talk to you alone, and I can never do that at your house."

"Well, what do you think we should do?" Rachel asked.

"I have no idea," Sara answered. "Even if the worst possible things were going on in that house, what could we do? We can't tell anyone. They would think we're just a couple of bored housewives with overactive imaginations. We have absolutely nothing to go on."

The two woman sat in silence for a while, each absorbed in their own thoughts. Rachel was impulsive, as her actions the other night had proved. When she had questions, she wanted immediate answers. She wanted to find out why that house affected her the way it did, and she wanted to find out now. Sara, on the other hand, was analytical. She never made a decision without looking at all the possibilities first. She was painstakingly methodical, and never rushed into anything. All she wanted right now, was to have this feeling go away. She wanted her piece of mind back.

"How about this," Sara suggested. "For the next couple of weeks, lets just watch for signs of something, and I don't mean sneaking up to the house to peek in the windows."

"Okay, okay," Rachel agreed, slightly embarrassed. "Believe me, I don't want to go through that again either."

"All right, then," Sara said, with relief. "For the next couple of weeks, when we go for our walks, we'll look for any sign of something unusual. But, when Christie is with us, you'll have to keep your comments to yourself."

"I will, I don't want her involved in this at all. But let's change the direction we go, so that the two of us are alone when we go by there."

"Well, if you and I started at my house, we could go up Sunrise, over Rocky Ridge, and then pick up Christie. But, how are we going to justify you coming all the way over here by yourself?"

"I don't know, but I'll think of something."

"Rachel, this sounds so crazy. Maybe we really *are* just bored housewives looking for something to make our lives exciting?"

"Sara, if we wanted excitement, I'm sure we could think of something a lot more pleasant than this. I wasn't going to tell you this, but I've been dreaming about my mother for the past few nights. She's been warning me that my family is in danger, and that I'd better do something before it's too late."

"Oh, come on Rachel. Let's not get carried away."

"I know you don't believe in that kind of thing, but the dreams have felt so real, that they really scare me."

Chapter 25

He went back to the woods near Bobby's house, around 10:00 o'clock, and parked near the end of the street where there were no houses. As he got out of the van, he took a small penlight flashlight. He wanted to be able to see where he was going, but not have the light visible from any of the surrounding houses.

As he crept into the woods, he headed in the direction of the path he had seen the week before. The woods were very dense, which was what he had hoped for. Finally, he came upon what had to be the path. It was about eight to ten feet wide, and covered with leaves. Although trees and brush grew along either side, the path itself was clear from one street to the next. It was as though it had been purposely cleared at one time, and remained that way through years of use.

He walked along the path towards Bobby's street, and about half way down, he stopped and turned off his flashlight. He stood there looking around, and when he didn't see any light from the houses on either street, he realized that this area must also be hidden from view in the daytime. He turned on his light, and saw that there were large trees and dense brush on both sides. The area was perfect. He would have to take some chances, but it could work.

As he drove home, he went over the plan in his mind,. It was risky. If Bobby wasn't alone, or there were other people in the woods, he hoped he would be able to keep out of sight, because it would be hard to explain his presence there. He had never wanted to take chances before, but every time he thought about Frankie, he knew that he had to do it. This cruel child would not get away from him this time.

The next week went by quickly for him. He went over his plan down to the smallest detail, and assembled all of the supplies he would need. He bought camouflaged clothes at the Army and Navy store, so that he could more easily remain hidden in the woods, and a pair of heavy work gloves. He had the chloroform, the airtight container, and the rag he would use. He had the nylon rope, the duct tape, and most importantly the 50-lb. test fishing line, the strongest he could find. Each night, he would line them up in the order in which he would use them, and go over his plan again. By the time Saturday morning had arrived, he was confident that he would not be coming home alone.

As he drove to the park, he started to have doubts. What if someone saw him carrying the boy to his van, or even worse, putting him inside. He could always say that he found him lying unconscious in the woods, and was bringing him to the hospital. By the time they discovered why the boy was unconscious, he would be gone. He decided not to worry about something that might never happen. After all, his mission was so important, that he had to take chances.

He timed himself so that he would arrive at the park at around 12:30. He wanted to be sure Bobby was still there, but didn't want to have to wait too long. He drove by the park, and was alarmed when he didn't see the boys in their usual place. Then he noticed some boys at the snack bar, so he pulled into the parking lot. He relaxed a little when he saw Bobby with the other boys, but was still disturbed by the possibility that he was going to eat something here, and not go home for lunch. He was relieved when he noticed that the boys only got something to drink, and then headed back to the jumps they had constructed.

He left the parking lot, and drove to the wooded area he had visited the week before. He drove to the end of the street, and backed the van as far into the woods as he could, hoping it would not be visible from the street.

He put the container with the chloroform soaked rag in one pocket, and the fishing line in the other. When he went into the woods, he found the path easily in the daylight. He followed the path to the street he had driven down, and looked in the direction he had parked. When he looked closely, he could see the van between the trees, but he was satisfied that Bobby would not notice it. He walked back down the path, and started preparing for Bobby's arrival.

He took the fishing line out of his pocket, and tied one end around a tree at the edge of the path, about two feet from the ground. He unwound the line, and laid it across the path. Holding the other end in his hand, he crouched behind a dense bush directly on the other side. He wound the line around one gloved hand, and pulled back with both hands. The line snapped up, and stretched almost invisibly across the path. He pulled as hard as he could, until he was satisfied that the line would hold. He went to the other side of the path, positioning the line along the ground again, and covering it with leaves. When he reached the bush, he wound the line around his hand, crouched down again, and waited. As he waited he thought about Frankie, and how happy he would be when there was no one to torment him. How he wished that when he was a boy, there had been someone to get rid of his own tormentors. Someone like him.

Bobby said goodbye to his friends, and headed home for lunch. He rode as fast as he could, because he didn't want to be late. He had been late coming home from a friend's house yesterday, and his mother had been worried. She told him that if he was late today, he wouldn't be able to ride his bike tomorrow. She had also said that she didn't like him taking the shortcut through the woods, but he had to do it today if he was going to make it home on time. He slowed down enough to make the turn into the woods, and then sped up again. He suddenly felt a slight tug, and then his bike jerked to a stop. He went flying over the handlebars, flew about ten feet through the air, and landed on his back in the middle of the path. Miraculously he wasn't hurt, but he had the wind knocked out of him, and laid there trying to catch his breath. When he opened his eyes, he saw a familiar face staring down at him.

Susan Biscoe

He saw Bobby coming down the path. In the time he
had been waiting here, he hadn't seen another person,
luckily Bobby was also alone. When the boy had first
come into the woods, he was going too slow, but to the
man's relief he began to pedal faster. When the boy
had almost reached him, he pulled on the line with all
his might. The line caught the bike just under the
handlebars. The man held on as tight as he could, as
the line began to stretch forward. He was sure it was
going to break, when all at once the bike jerked to a
stop. The boy went flying over the handlebars,
flipped in the air, and landed on his back. The man
rushed over to where the boy had landed, and stood
over him. Although the boy's eyes were closed, he was
moving slightly as he tried to catch his breath. The
man took the chloroform soaked rag from it's
container, and saw the boy open his eyes just before
he bent down, and held the cloth over his face.

When he was sure that Bobby was unconscious, he
went back to where the bike had landed, and untangled
the fishing line. He cut off the end he had tied to
the tree, and stuffed the line into his pocket. He
went back to where he had been hiding, and made sure
he had not left anything behind. He then took a
branch, and brushed the area around the bush, to erase
any trace that he had been there. He went back to
where Bobby was lying, and with great effort, lifted
him over his shoulder. He walked through the dense
woods to where he had left the van, and after making
sure that there was no one else around, opened the
back and placed the unconscious boy inside. He bound
the boy's hands and feet with the nylon rope, and put
duct tape over his mouth. He pulled the van out of
the woods, and headed toward the interstate. He was
sure at any moment that he would see the lights of a
police cruiser in his rear view mirror, and didn't
begin to relax until he was halfway home.

When he realized that he had gotten away with it,
he couldn't believe how easy it had been. Everything
had gone perfectly, down to the smallest detail. The
only real moment of fear he had was when he thought
the line wasn't going to hold, but it did. Bobby was

now safely stowed in the back of the van, and he couldn't hurt Frankie any more. All he had to do now was figure out how to make Bobby suffer, the way he had made Frankie suffer. Make them suffer, and then eliminate them. That was his mission, his only reason for existing, and no one could stop him.

Chapter 26

When Rachel left Sara's house that day, she had felt vindicated. Although she had been anxious to do more than just watch for something unusual, at least she now felt that she had an ally. Sara had always been so sensible, that for her to have even the slightest feeling that there might be something going on in that house, was significant.

Rachel was relieved that Sara also wanted to exclude Christie from their "investigation", and was trying to figure out how they were going to do that, when Christie provided her with the solution. Later that same afternoon, Christie had called to tell Rachel that she had tripped over some of the toys her son had left on the floor, and sprained her ankle.

Of course, the doctor had told Christie it was the worst sprain he had ever seen, and she was going to have to stay off of her foot completely for a couple of weeks. Her mother-in-law was going to come and stay with them, to take care of Jimmy, while Scott was at work. Rachel knew that Christie was milking this for all that she could, and for the first time since she had met her, she was grateful for Christie's need to be the center of attention. This meant that she obviously would not be walking with them for a while. She had sympathized with Christie for a few minutes, hung up the phone, and immediately called Sara.

That evening, although it was only a few streets away, Rachel had driven over to Sara's to begin their walk. She didn't want either of them to have to walk home alone. For the next two weeks, they walked by the house on Rocky Ridge, looking for anything unusual. They even altered their usual route so that they could walk by the house twice, coming first from one direction, than the other.

The first thing they noticed were the lights attached to each corner of the house.

"I don't think they were there before," Sara stated. "I never looked at the house too closely, but I'm sure I would have noticed them."

"I *have* looked closely, and I know they weren't there," Rachel agreed. "And besides, those lights have motion detectors. If they were there before, they would have come on the night I went up to the house.

"Well, there's nothing really unusual about motion detector lights. We both have them, a lot of people do."

"That may be true, but we have them at our back doors, and in the back yard, not on every corner of the house."

Sara looked at the house again, and realized that Rachel was right. There were lights on both of the front corners, and the one back corner that she could see. When they walked back from the other direction, she noticed a fourth one at the other back corner. Nothing sinister about it really, but strange just the same.

"It's a good thing those lights *weren't* there the night you made your daring excursion into enemy territory," Sara joked "It would have been like getting caught in the searchlights during a prison breakout."

Rachel felt a chill go down her back as she imagined herself crouched a few feet in front of this house, caught in the glare of the lights.

"This may sound a little paranoid, but I wonder if those lights were installed *because* of what I did that night."

"It doesn't sound paranoid to me. It's actually pretty logical. Those dogs did go crazy that night. Maybe he was afraid someone was trying to break in, so he got some security lights."

"A bit of 'overkill' don't you think? Three rottweilers make for a pretty good security system. What could be so valuable that he had to put the lights all the way around the house to protect it?"

"All right, I admit it's strange," Sara confessed. "But it's still not enough to go running to the police with. I can just see us now, 'But officer, he has security lights AND dogs. Isn't that enough for a search warrant?'"

"Don't be a smart ass Sara, I'm not saying that. I'm only saying that it's something. At least it's more than just having the hairs on the back of my neck stand up when I walk by the place."

For the next week, the women walked at their usual time, after dinner. They didn't see anything else that they considered unusual, and were beginning to think that they were wasting their time, when Rachel had an idea.

"Why don't we change the times that we walk? We always go by there at the same time every day. Maybe we should go later, like one night start at eight o'clock, the next at seven, the next at nine. Maybe even later."

"It's a good idea, Rachel, but how are we going to explain our unusual schedule to our husbands? They'll think we're nuts."

"I can tell Michael that I'm tired of having to clean up from dinner, after I get home, so I'm not going for my walk until later."

"Okay, I'll just tell Scott that I have to wait until you're ready. Just come over every night when you think the time is right."

For the next week, the women varied the times they would walk past the house on Rocky Ridge. They didn't know what they expected to see, but they were hypersensitive to every movement that they saw, and sound that they heard. Sometimes they would see just a shadow of some kind of vehicle parked near the back of the house. They assumed it was the same dark van they had seen the night they had looked over Sara's back fence. Although they would have liked to have tried to get a look from that vantage point again, they were afraid the dogs would sound an alarm, and then they would have to explain what they were doing there to Scott.

At times they would see light coming from around the edges of the heavy drapes covering the picture window, but most of time the house was completely dark. This seemed unusual to both of them, especially when they could tell that a vehicle was parked there. No matter what time they walked by, they never saw a single person coming, or going from the house.

Toward the end of the second week, they began to doubt that there was anything strange about the house at all. Maybe the person who lived there was just a loner who went to bed early, and had no friends, or social life. They considered going back to their old routine of walking right after dinner, but the fact that Christie didn't like to walk after dark, made them decide not to. This way, when her ankle was better, she still would not be walking with them, and that by itself made this new routine preferable. They continued to look at the house when they went by, but not as closely as they had before. They laughed at themselves, and how carried away they had gotten just because this house didn't look like all the others.

The strange feeling Sara had experienced on that day, two weeks before, had completely vanished. She decided that she was probably just extra sensitive that morning, because she had almost confronted Rachel about Amanda. She was glad that she had avoided that. She knew how much she would resent it if someone tried to tell her how to raise her kids, and Rachel was even touchier about that than she was. If Rachel wanted to talk to her about it she would, and until then Sara would just keep her mouth shut.

Rachel also didn't get the feeling as often, when she walked by the house. The hairs on the back of her neck would still prickle occasionally, but she tried to ignore it. Her life finally seemed to be going the way she wanted it to, and she didn't want her stupid imagination to ruin the contentment she was feeling. The only thing that really bothered Rachel was that she was still having the same dream about her mother. Sometimes they would be standing in the middle of a playground, surrounded by children playing. Sometimes they would be at a baseball field, and sometimes they would even be standing in front of the house on Rocky Ridge. Although the setting in the dreams would change, her mother's words were always the same.

"Be careful Rachel, your family is in danger. You have to stop him before it's too late."

Chapter 27

He brought Bobby into the house under the cover of darkness, just as he had done with all of the others. After he had dumped him on the mattress, and locked the door securely, he went back up the stairs. As he sat in the living room, in the dark, he thought again about how easy it had been. Why had he ever wasted his time with the dog? This way was so much better. He didn't have the inconvenience of having to go to the pound first, and then returning the dog later. It was more dangerous this way, but also more thrilling. He felt much more powerful than he ever had before. After all he had just snatched this boy up, within 150 yards from his own house, and no one had stopped him.

Since he didn't have to give the boy a second dose of chloroform, as he had with the others, he knew he would be waking up sooner too. That was good. He wasn't sure yet exactly what he was going to do, but at least he didn't have to wait long to see the fear on the boy's face. Like the fear he had seen on Frankie's face, that day on the baseball field. Fear, suffering, and then elimination. That was this cruel child's future. His only future.

He got up to turn on the news. Maybe there would be something about Bobby's disappearance. On his way to the TV, he glanced out of the window, and noticed two people walking by his house. It was unusual to see people out walking at this time of night. As he looked closer he recognized Amanda's mother. She was with the woman that lived behind him. He wondered where the third one was, and why they were out this late. They both turned to look at his house as they went by, and even though he knew they couldn't see him, he backed away from the window.

During the past two weeks, he had been so preoccupied with his plans for Bobby, that he hadn't thought about anything else. He now realized that he hadn't seen these women during the usual time they would walk by. He had just taken it for granted that it would be safe to bring the boy into the house after dark, because no one would be around then. What if they had been walking by when he had been taking Bobby out of the van. Although it was dark, they might have been able to see something. He had been very lucky tonight, but he wouldn't take any more chances. He would be much more careful in the future. He turned on the TV, and went back to the couch. The news was just starting, but he was too exhausted to keep his eyes open. He closed them, and within five minutes, he was sound asleep.

Bobby opened his eyes. At least he thought he opened them. It was so dark, he couldn't tell. He tried to stretch, and felt a dull ache throughout his entire body. It felt like he had the flu or something. He remembered falling off of his bike, and then seeing someone standing over him, but he didn't remember a thing after that. He wondered where he was. He knew it wasn't home, because the bed was too hard.

"I must be in the hospital," he said, out loud. "I guess I got hurt worse than I thought."

He wanted to call for the nurse, but he couldn't find the call button. It hurt too much, when he tried to get up, so he decided to go back to sleep. His mother and father would be there in the morning anyway. Although he hurt all over, he didn't think anything was broken. He could probably go home when his parents got there. Maybe he would be able to get out of going to school for a couple of days.

When he woke up it was daylight, and he cursed himself for falling asleep. He knew Bobby must have woken up by now, and he had wanted to be there when he did. He wanted to see the look on his face when he opened his eyes, and realized what had happened. He went down the stairs, and unlocked the door. When he entered the room, he didn't turn on the overhead light. The dim light filtering in around the edges of the only window was enough to see the room clearly. He expected to see the boy sitting up, or walking *around, but he was still lying there with his eyes closed.*

He must be dead, he thought with alarm. The chloroform would have worn off hours ago, so something had to be wrong. Maybe there had been some kind of hidden injuries, and he had died during the night. He didn't feel sad, or even disappointed, but he felt cheated. The boy was supposed to experience the same fear and suffering he had inflicted, and now he was dead. Just when he thought his plans were working out perfectly, something always went wrong. Then Bobby moved a little, and he heard him groan. HE WAS ALIVE! Everything was going to be all right. He hadn't blown this one, after all. He would get it right this time.

He walked over, and stood over the boy, as he had done after he had fallen off of the bike. When Bobby looked up, he looked into a face that seemed strange and familiar at the same time.

"Are you the doctor?" he asked.

The man stood there for a few minutes, not sure what to say, or if he should say anything at all. He had expected to see fear on the boy's face, and so far he had only seen confusion.

"What makes you think I'm a doctor?" he replied.

"Well, isn't this the hospital? I had an accident on my bike."

"You really are stupid, aren't you. Does this look like a hospital to you?"

Bobby was confused by the man's words. Why was he calling him stupid? A doctor wouldn't do that. And if this wasn't a hospital, where was he, and how did he get here? He looked around the room, and realized that it was definitely not a hospital room. It was dirty, and he wasn't on a hospital bed, it was just a dirty mattress on the floor. He looked back up into the man's face.

"I know you from somewhere don't I?" he asked. "Who are you?"

"I guess you might say I'm a protector. A protector, and a punisher. Someone has to protect innocent children like Frankie, from cruel children like you. And punish you for your cruelty."

When he said he was a punisher, he saw a flicker of the look he wanted to see cross Bobby's face. He was still mostly confused, but the fear was there, just below the surface.

"What are you going to do?" Bobby asked warily.

"You don't want to know. You really don't," he said with a chuckle.

Then he turned, and left the room. As he turned the key, the dead bolt slid loudly into place. He decided to leave him alone for the rest of the day, and let him think about what he had said. Sometimes the imagination of a little boy, can be much worse than the real thing, and he wanted to let him imagine what was going to happen next. He knew that the next time he saw the boy, he would see more than just a flicker of fear on his face.

Chapter 28

Rachel and Sara were so involved in their conversation, as they walked along Rocky Ridge, that they didn't even look at the house the first time they went by it. In a couple of weeks, school would be out for the summer. They were planning all of the things that they wanted to do with their families, like taking several day trips to interesting places. They both loved the ocean, so they also wanted to rent a house together, for a week or two that was on the shore. They knew it would not be easy to convince their husbands though, because Michael liked the mountains, and Scott preferred a lake, so he could fish.

"If we go somewhere like Cape Cod, with fresh water lakes nearby, that would satisfy Scott," Sara suggested. "But, I don't know what to do about Michael. I don't know of any place that has mountains along the shoreline."

"To be honest Sara, I think Michael would be just as happy if we went without him. He would love to have a week or two at home alone, being able to do whatever he wanted."

"Hey, that's an idea. Maybe we can take the kids ourselves. I think if I tell Scott that we're going to the ocean he might be happy to stay home too."

"Now that would be a vacation," Rachel said.

Sara could hear the excitement in Rachel's voice.

"Do you think the guys would really go for it?" she asked.

"Let's mention it to them tomorrow. We have to make plans soon if we're ever going to find a place to rent that's big enough for all of us."

The women had been so engrossed in their vacation plans, and they were far enough past the house, that they never noticed the dark van with it's lights out, pulling into the driveway behind them.

Sara didn't usually go over to Rachel's for coffee on the weekends, but this morning was different. As she came in the door, she yelled, "Rachel, are you busy?"

Rachel came into the kitchen, with the vacuum cleaner hose in her hand.

"Extremely, but please interrupt me," she joked. "What's up?"

"Did you see the news this morning?"

"No, I haven't even looked at the newspaper yet? Why?"

"Not the newspaper, there was a bulletin on TV. There's another child missing."

"What! Where? When did it happen?"

"A town about fifty miles west of here. It happened yesterday. This time it's a nine year old boy."

"Oh no. Are there any details?"

"Just that he was on his way home from a playground near his house, and he never made it home. They found his bike in some woods between the playground and his house, but there was no sign of him."

"Sara, this is horrible. They still don't have any leads on that little girl that disappeared a few weeks ago, and now another one. What's wrong with this world?"

"I know, they showed a picture of the little boy on TV. He looked so cute in his baseball uniform. All I could think of was Joey."

"Baseball uniform? And did you say he was on his way home from a playground?"

"That's right. What's wrong Rachel?"

Rachel was trying to remember. What was it about a baseball field, and a playground? And then it hit her. Her dreams. The dreams about her mother. Sometimes they were at a playground, and sometimes they were in the middle of a baseball field. And sometimes they were standing in front of the house on Rocky Ridge!

This was just too weird. It couldn't be true. As much as she had felt there was something creepy about that house, she never in a million years would have thought it could have something to do with this. IT

CAN'T! she silently chided herself. It's just you're warped imagination, again.

"Rachel, what's wrong?" Sara repeated.

"Oh, nothing," Rachel said, distractedly, "I was just thinking about those poor kids, and their families. I don't think I'd survive if one of my kids were missing."

"Neither would I," Sara agreed. "It has to be the worst possible thing that can happen to anyone. Even though they say that they still haven't found a connection, I bet that all of these disappearances are related. I hope they find this psychopath soon. No one is going to be safe until they do."

Chapter 29

After the man was gone, Bobby sat there trying to understand what was happening. The last thing he remembered was feeling his bike jerk beneath him, and then flying over the handlebars. He had landed hard, but he had thought he was okay. Then he saw a man standing over him, that man. Then he smelled something funny, and that was it until he woke up here. That man must have brought him to this place, but why? He hadn't made any sense before, talking about cruel children, and punishment. He had even called himself a punisher. That had sounded really lame, but the look in his eyes when he said it had made Bobby afraid. And what was that bit about Frankie? He had said that he had to protect Frankie. Frankie who? Protect him from what? Bobby just didn't get it.

He got up and started to look around the room he was in. This had to be in the basement of some place. He could tell by the small window up near the ceiling. He pulled the only chair in the room over to the window, and stood on it. Even if he could fit through it, it was way too high for him to reach. He knew that the door was locked, but he tried it anyway. This was really weird. What did this guy want with him? He looked harmless enough, except for that look he had gotten when he had called himself a punisher.

He decided he would wait until dark, before he went down to see Bobby again. Something about the darkness always made the fear come easier. When he walked into the room, Bobby was sitting cross-legged on the mattress. He walked in and carefully locked the door with his key. He wasn't going to take any chances this time.

As he came into the room, Bobby said, "You were there when I fell off my bike, weren't you?"

"Of course I was," he chuckled. "You wouldn't have fallen if I wasn't."

Bobby looked at the man curiously. What did he mean by that? He couldn't have had anything to do with it. He didn't even see this guy until after he had fallen.

"You look a little confused Bobby, let me explain. I've been watching you for quite a while. I've seen the things you've said and done to other innocent children, and I know exactly what you are."

"I don't know what you're talking about," Bobby replied."I haven't done anything."

"Really? I'm sure Frankie would disagree."

"Why do you keep talking about Frankie? Who is Frankie?"

"YOU KNOW DAMN WELL WHO FRANKIE IS!" he shouted.

Bobby cringed back against the wall. This man didn't look so harmless anymore.

"Do you mean Frankie Shepard?" he asked timidly. "From my baseball team?"

The man stood there for a few minutes, with his eyes blazing. Bobby didn't know if he had heard him, but he was afraid to ask again. Finally the man spoke, and Bobby was surprised by the hatred he heard in his voice.

"Yes, Frankie from YOUR baseball team. Frankie who not only can't catch, but can't even run. Frankie with the piece of junk for a bike, who should go home and play with his sister's dolls, because he's too fat and stupid to do anything else."

Bobby's head was starting to hurt. Who was this guy? How did he know all this stuff? Did Frankie tell him?

"Are you his uncle, or something?" Bobby asked.

"I told you I'm his protector, and your punisher."

There was that look again. It was kind of happy, and kind of crazy at the same time. Bobby didn't know what it meant, but it scared him.

"Look, I'm sorry," he said. "I know I said some mean things to him, and I'm really sorry. If you let me go, I promise I'll never do it again."

He looked at Bobby strangely. He had never heard one of them say that they were sorry before. Never. Was it possible?

"If I let you go, will you be nice to other children from now on?"

"Yes, yes I promise." Bobby answered.

Thank God! He was going to let him go.

"Okay, but I'm going to have to tie you up, and blindfold you first."

"Why?" Bobby asked, warily.

"So you can't identify where you were taken, and that way no one will be able to find me."

Bobby didn't want to be tied up, but he wanted to go home, so he agreed. As soon as I get home I'll make sure that they catch this wacko, and put him away forever, he thought.

He tied Bobby's feet together, and then stretched the rope tightly and tied his hands together, so that the boy would not be able to raise his hands above his waist. He tied a rag over his eyes, and then put a piece of duct tape across his mouth.

The boy really thought that he had bought his pathetic act, and he was going to bring him home. What a joke. Hadn't he already decided that they couldn't change? That they had to be eliminated? Fear, suffering, elimination. That was his mission. He had already succeeded with the fear. He had seen it on the boy's face. He had thought long and hard about how to make him suffer, and then the answer had come to him. It was so simple.

He carried the boy out to the van, and put him into the small rubber boat that was inside. In the boat he had already placed the tarp, chains, and cinder blocks. It was after midnight now, so he knew it was safe. He drove to the deserted access road, and parked. He pulled the boat, and it's contents out of the van, and dragged it down to the pond. The boy was struggling against his bonds now, obviously realizing he was not on his way home.

Bobby was starting to panic. He had thought it was strange when he had taped his mouth, but then this guy was strange anyway. Now he knew something was wrong. He had put him in the back of some kind of truck, and only driven for a short time. When they stopped,

Bobby had expected him to lift him out.   Instead he
had pulled out whatever he had put him in, and was
dragging it somewhere. He didn't know what he was in,
but there was some kind of rocks in there with him.
He kept bumping up against them, and scraping his
arms. When he heard rushing water somewhere nearby,
he knew he wasn't anywhere near home.

*When they got to the edge of the pond, he took the
tarp out of the boat, and spread it on the ground.   He
set out a flashlight, so he could see what he was
doing, lifted the struggling boy out, and placed him
on the tarp.*
*"Lie still," he commanded, as he backhanded Bobby
across the face, "or I'll slit your throat."*
*The boy immediately stopped moving. He wrapped the
tarp around him, but unlike the others, he left his
head out.   He wanted to see his face.   He tied the
tarp around the boy, put him back into the boat, and
secured the cinder blocks to the tarp.   Then he
paddled out into the water.*
*When he got to the deepest part of the pond, he
removed the boys blindfold, and shined the flashlight
onto his face. When he saw the fear in his eyes, he
smiled.*
*"Did you really think I fell for that act?" he
whispered, viciously. "I know you.   I know what you
are, and I know that you can't change. You don't even
want to.   You made Frankie suffer, and now it's your
turn to suffer."*
*He pushed the boy, and the cinder blocks, into the
water, and watched them sink.   He imagined the boy
trying to hold his breath.   As he saw the bubbles
rising to the surface, he imagined the water rushing
into his nose, and the burning feeling he must be
experiencing, as it entered his lungs.*

"*Suffering*," he whispered. "*He's suffering now.*"

When the bubbles stopped, he knew it was over, and that Frankie was safe.

Chapter 30

It was a warm day for June, the temperature already in the lower 80's. Rachel and Sara were sitting on Sara's deck, with an iced pitcher of lemonade, watching the kids splash around in the pool.

"Sara, promise me that if you get tired of having me and my kids, over here this summer, that you'll tell me. The kids love your pool, and just watching them makes me feel cooler."

"I'm not going to get tired of you, Rachel. I love having the company. My kids are getting to the age now that they don't want 'Mom' hanging around all the time anyway."

"I don't think Brian will ever get to that age. He wants me around all the time."

"Well enjoy it while you can. Believe me, it doesn't last, and I really miss it."

Rachel gazed over at Brian, in the pool. The other kids, Amanda, Sara's sons, and their friends, were all splashing around, and having a great time. Brian, on the other hand, was sitting on a float with his feet dangling in the water, just watching them. Rachel knew that if she was in the pool, Brian would be jumping in, swimming around, and having a great time with her. Why, she wondered, is he so outgoing with me, and so shy with other kids?

Brian sat on the float, watching the other kids. He didn't like the games the other boys played in the pool, like who could make the biggest splash, or Marco Polo. He wasn't very good at those games, and could never win. He wished Taran, Joey, and their friends would go somewhere else. Then he could probably get his mother to come in the pool. But, as long as there were so many other kids here, he knew his mother would think he didn't need her in the pool with him.

Amanda was having a great time. Brian would usually be complaining about them splashing him, or something else just as annoying, but today he wasn't saying a word. Amanda thought it was because Taran and Joey's friends were here, and Brian didn't know them.   She didn't really care what the reason was. School was out, her Mom had said they would probably be spending a lot of time at Aunt Sara's, and it looked like it was going to be a great summer.

The older boys climbed out of the pool, and Taran's friend suggested that they go ride their bikes on the trails through the woods.

"Mom," Taran yelled over to his mother, "Can we ride our bikes on the trails for a while?"

"NO!" Sara responded, a little too sharply. "I'm sorry," she said immediately, "But, I don't want you in the woods until they catch this guy."

"Awe Mom," Taran complained. "Nothing is going to happen with the four of us together."

"Tell that to the families of those three little boys in Tennessee. They were together too."

Taran could tell from the tone of his mother's voice that it would do no good to argue with her.

"Let's just stay here," he said to his friends, as he jumped back in the pool. "It's too hot to ride our bikes anyway."

They don't have any leads on those missing kids, do they?" Rachel asked, with concern.

"If they do, they're not saying. Do you think I'm being over protective? I mean, all of those disappearances did happen a long way from here."

"No way," Rachel said "I'm going to tell you something, and I want you to convince me that I'm not crazy."

"I always think you're crazy," Sara joked.

"I'm serious Sara, because I'm beginning to think that I am."

Sara looked at her friend closely, and realized that she *was* serious. A feeling of dread descended on her. She didn't really want to hear what Rachel had to say, but knew that she would.

"What is it?" she asked warily.

"Do you remember when I told you about the dreams I've been having?"

"About your mother?"

"Yes, the ones where she was trying to warn me about something. Well I didn't tell you this part, but I swear it's true, in the dreams we are either standing in a playground, in the middle of a baseball field, or in front of that house on Rocky Ridge."

Sara started to tell Rachel it was all just a coincidence, but when she felt a chill go down her back, she stopped. Instead she asked, "When did you start having the dreams?"

"About a month ago," Rachel answered, and seeing the look on Sara's face, she added, "That's right, the last little boy was last seen at a playground, and from the picture they're showing, he also plays baseball. I didn't know any of that until a few days ago."

"Rachel, are you saying that you think the person who lives in that house is responsible for these missing kids?" Sara asked skeptically.

"I don't know," Rachel sighed. "I just can't figure out why I've been dreaming about playgrounds, and baseball fields. I could understand if my dreams were always in front of that house. I could attribute that to my imagination, but why the playground and baseball field? Sara the only time I've ever been to a baseball field was to watch your son play."

"Well, lets think about this for a minute. You would naturally associate playgrounds with children, so that could still be your unconscious at work. The only time you've been at a ball field was when Joey was playing, so you could associate baseball fields with kids too. Besides none of these kids were taken from those two places, they were all either in front of their own houses, or on the way home."

"I guess you're right," Rachel admitted. "You must think I'm really deranged."

"Of course I don't. Something like this puts everyone off balance, especially when you have kids like we do."

Rachel looked across the yard, at the children. They were having such a good time together in the pool. They were all so innocent. Questions began swirling around in her head. Why do they have to grow up in a world where they have to be afraid of some maniac snatching them away?

What kind of a person could hurt an innocent child? How could someone get away with this for so long? She looked towards the house on Rocky Ridge, barely visible through the trees. Why can't I get over this obsession? she thought, and then jumped at the sound of Sara's voice.

"You are jittery today, aren't you?" Sara laughed.

"I'm sorry, I guess I was in my own world. Did you say something?"

"I said, let's go make some lunch for the kids."

"Oh, sure. Do you want me to go home, and get anything?"

"I have plenty of peanut butter and jelly," Sara answered "Are you sure you're all right? You look so, I don't know, distracted."

"I'm fine," Rachel insisted. "Peanut butter and jelly for six, right?"

"Hey guys, do you want some lunch?" Sara yelled to her son's friends. When they both nodded, Sara turned and said, "Peanut butter and jelly for six."

As they went into the house, Rachel looked back at the house through the trees. She thought she caught a glimpse of a figure in the upstairs window, but when she looked more closely, it was gone.

"You're really losing it now," she muttered to herself.

While they prepared the sandwiches, Rachel and Sara tried to concentrate on more pleasant subjects.

"Why don't we take the kids to the Water Park at High Peak, this summer," Sara suggested.

"That sounds good," Rachel agreed "And, we can take them to the amusement park over in Westwood, too."

"Did you talk to Michael yet about renting a house at the beach?"

"No, I haven't really had the chance. Did you mention it?"

"Not yet. Why don't we split a pizza for dinner, and we can ambush them both at the same time."

"Good idea, kind of like strength in numbers."

"Right, the six of us against the two of them."

"The *six* of us?"

"You, me, and the kids. They won't have a chance."

"Well if Amanda likes the idea, I know Michael won't fight it. She can wrap him around her little finger."

"Good, we need all the advantages that we can get."

Rachel and Sara brought the sandwiches out to the deck, and called the kids out of the pool for lunch. Sara warned them to stay out of the pool for at least an hour after they ate, or they would get cramps.

"We'll be in the house if you need us." she told them.

When the two women were inside, Rachel said, "They don't really have to wait an hour you know. That's an old wives' tale."

"I know," Sara said, with a wink. "But it will give us a chance to watch our Soap."

"Maybe those old wives knew what they were doing." Rachel laughed.

Rachel had called home, and left a message on their answering machine, telling Michael to come over to the Spencer's after he got home. She said that they were going to split a pizza for dinner, and to bring his bathing suit if he wanted to cool off in the pool.

Scott looked really wiped out when he came home, and didn't look too pleased to see a bunch of kids running around the back yard.

"Maybe we should leave," Rachel offered.

"Are you crazy?" Sara asked. "This is perfect. The more commotion the better. If Scott thinks that this is what he has to look forward to all summer, he'll be happy to get rid of us for a week or two."

"Sara, I never knew that you were so devious."

When Scott came out, he was in his bathing suit. He grunted a "hello" to Rachel, and headed for the pool. Michael showed up a few minutes later, and joined Scott in the water.

"We're going to pick up the pizza." Sara yelled.

"Do you both have to go?" Scott asked, eyeing the yard full of kids.

"You can handle them for fifteen minutes," Sara said.

As soon as they were in the car, Sara looked at Rachel with a broad smile on her face, and said, "Something tells me that our suggestion will be met with a minimum of opposition."

After they had finished eating, Rachel and Sara went into the house to make some more lemonade. As Sara filled the pitcher with water, Rachel asked, "Did you hear about Angela Cooper?"

"You mean about her going to Tricia's house? Taran told me about it. Don't you think her parents overreacted a little? I mean, grounding her totally for a month."

"Actually, no I don't," Rachel replied. "I think I'd do the same thing, and take away her phone privileges too!"

Sara glanced at Rachel, trying to figure out if she was serious. She hated getting into these discussions with her. When it came to disciplining kids, their views were so different, and Rachel had a way of making her feel like she was way too lenient if she didn't agree with her.

Just then Michael walked into the kitchen, with Scott.

"So, what are we talking about?" he asked.

"Angela Cooper," Rachel answered. "Sara thinks her parents overreacted when they grounded her for a month."

"What did she do?" Scott asked.

He hadn't heard anything about it, because Sara never, ever discussed other what other kids did with her husband. Their views on discipline were even further apart than Sara's and Rachel's, and he would totally embarrass his sons by bringing up whatever had happened when the other child was around.

"Angela lied to her parents about where she was going," Rachel began explaining, as Sara groaned inwardly. "She said she was going to Lindsay's house, and she went to Tricia's instead."

"Why would she lie," Scott asked, looking more interested by the minute. He knew the Coopers, and saw them occasionally at Little League games.

"Because she knew her parents wouldn't let her go to Tricia's house after school. Both of her parents work, and there's no supervision."

"God Rachel, the girl is 13 years old." Michael said, "It's not like she needs a baby sitter or something. I can't wait until Amanda is that old."

"You would say that. Anything to make *your* life easier," Rachel replied, scornfully. "I happen to think a 13 year old girl needs just as much supervision as a nine year old. For different reasons maybe, but just as much."

"I was baby sitting when I was 12 years old," Sara interjected. "You can't get less supervision than that. So, what's the big deal about two 13 year olds being alone for a few hours."

"Yeah, but were you having sex when you were twelve?" Rachel questioned. "Thirteen year old girls today are. You can't compare the two Sara, it's different today."

"And I know the reason it's different," Scott announced. "It's permissive parents like Sara that are the problem."

"EXCUSE ME!" Sara said, raising her voice.

"It's true," Scott continued, ignoring the fury on Sara's face. "When I was a kid, if you misbehaved you got a slap upside the head. It made you think twice before you did it again, believe me. Today, if you give your kid a swat on the butt, you get accused of child abuse."

"Your answer to everything is 'a swat'," Sara replied, acidly. "Clean up your room, SWAT! Do your homework, SWAT! Finish your brussel sprouts, SWAT! I happen to believe that hitting a child, for any reason, is wrong. All you're teaching them is that if someone doesn't do what you want them to do, hit them."

"That may be true, Sara," Rachel said. "But, you have to have some discipline, otherwise the kids will grow up thinking they can do whatever they want."

"Of course there has to be consequences to their actions," Sara said, feeling the anger she had just experienced being replaced by a feeling of exasperation. "But, the punishment has to fit the crime. If Angela is grounded for a month for going to Tricia's house, what's the consequence going to be if she comes home drunk, or stoned?"

"Grounded for the rest of her life." Rachel answered.

"Boarding school?" Michael offered.

"A good beating." Scott said, with determination. "It worked for me. Fear is a powerful deterrent."

"And if fear is the only way you have to control your children, what happens when they're not afraid of you anymore?" Sara asked, glaring at her husband. "And, trust me, that day will come sooner than you think."

"My father instilled enough fear in me that I'm still afraid of him to this day, and he's been dead for five years." Scott answered.

"And tell me something Scott," Sara said, clenching her teeth, and feeling the anger rising in her again. "Did you turn out to be such a *perfect* individual that you *really* believe the way you were raised was the *right* way?"

"You know something," Michael said, feeling more uncomfortable by the minute. "This is like politics and religion. It should be off limits for a subject of conversation. Come on Scott, we have to get down to the lumber yard, and get those boards for the deck before they close."

Scott looked like he was about to say something else, and then without a word, he turned and followed Michael out the door.

"Wow," Rachel said, "I don't think I've ever seen you that mad."

"He makes me sick sometimes." Sara answered, the total disgust she was feeling was evident, and not only in the words she spoke, but the way she said them.

"Scott must know how strongly you feel about hitting kids. It was like he was deliberately goading you."

"I think he was. He probably figured if he did it in front of you and Michael, I wouldn't make a scene."

"Big mistake!" Rachel said, laughing.

Sara looked at Rachel for a long moment, as if she trying to figure something out. Then she said, "You think I'm too lenient with my kids too, don't you?"

"I guess sometimes I do," Rachel said carefully. She didn't want to make Sara angry again, but she felt that their friendship could survive a little honesty. "But, I know that you think I'm too strict."

With Amanda, anyway, Sara thought silently. Why was she such a coward that she couldn't say it out loud.

"I guess the reason we can have such different parenting styles," Rachel continued, "and still be friends, is because we don't try to tell each other how to raise our kids. It's different with husbands. For some reason they think they have a right to have a say in how their kids are brought up."

Sara glanced sharply at Rachel. Was she trying to say that Scott was right?

"I'm sorry," Rachel apologized, when she saw the look on Sara's face. "I didn't mean that the way it sounded, it was just my lame attempt at humor. You know the last thing I would do is defend Scott to you. As far as I'm concerned, husbands are never right."

Sara laughed, feeling the tension drain away.

"You know, no matter how angry I get, you can always make me laugh. I wish I could be as strong willed, and outspoken as you are."

"Trust me Sara, you don't. Sometimes it's like everything that comes into my head, immediately goes out of my mouth. It's not a virtue, it's a curse."

"Well, maybe it's your influence, or maybe it's just that Scott made me so damn mad, but I just decided something. I'm not asking him about renting a house at the beach, I'm telling him. And, I'm telling him that we're going without him."

Chapter 31

What was wrong with him? Why did he feel like this? He had succeeded in everything he had planned to do. He should be feeling contented, fulfilled, and satisfied, but he only felt empty. He didn't feel like he had accomplished a thing. Even thinking about Frankie didn't help.

Bobby's words kept coming back to him. He had said that he was sorry. He was sorry, and he'd never do it again. Of course he didn't believe him. He was just saying that so he would let him go, but what if he was wrong. What if he did mean it, and he really was going to change.

"NO!" he shouted into the empty room. "I WAS RIGHT! I AM RIGHT! THEY'LL NEVER CHANGE! THEY CAN'T CHANGE!"

The sound of children laughing drew him to the open window. At first it seemed as though they were back, the ones that had left him alone in the woods so many years ago, but he knew that was not possible. When he looked out of the window, he saw Brian. There were other children in the pool, laughing and having a good time, but his attention was drawn to Brian. He sat alone on a float, being ignored by the other children.

The sight of Brian, made him sad. He felt the tears running down his cheeks, and angrily brushed them away.

"I will not cry," he whispered.

He looked at Amanda laughing, and having fun with the other children. He remembered the last time he had seen her there, and felt the familiar anger. He welcomed it. It was better than the sadness, and much better than the emptiness. He pulled a chair over to the window, and put the earpiece into his ear. Frankie doesn't need me to protect him anymore, he thought, but maybe Brian still does. I'll have to watch for a while, and see.

After the children had eaten their lunch, they decided to play a game of basketball. One of the boys he had never seen before had asked Brian to join the game to make the sides even, but before he could even answer, Amanda had said, "Don't bother, he can't even dribble the ball, or reach the basket. I don't think you'd want him on your team, I know I don't want him on mine." Brian walked away, and sat on the steps alone, watching the other children playing their game.

After they had tired of the basketball game, the children discussed what they could do next. After several suggestions were shot down, they finally settled on a game of Hide and Seek. They were going to play in the wooded area at the back of the yard, which gave him an even better view of them. He watched them hide, as Amanda who had volunteered to be "It", leaned against a tree counting out loud. It brought back the painful memory of his first, and only, game of Hide and Seek. He pushed it away, as he had always done before.

Amanda caught Brian easily, and then it was his turn to be "It". Brian leaned against a tree, and began to count to himself.

"You have count out loud, stupid," Amanda yelled. "Don't you know anything?"

As Brian began to count out loud, the other children ran and hid. When he started to search for them, one by one they all came out of hiding, and touched the tree before he even saw them.

"You have to be it again," Amanda laughed.

"Why?" Brian asked. "I was it already. It's someone else's turn now."

"Brian you are such a jerk," Amanda answered. "You have to be it until you catch someone, everyone knows that."

"Then I'm not playing anymore, and I'm going to tell Mom," Brian threatened.

"So what else is new?" Amanda said, with disgust, "Go ahead, and cry to Mom like the baby you are."

As Brian walked back toward the house, one of the boys said, "Come on back Brian, I'll be it this time."

Brian turned, and looked like he might rejoin the group, when Amanda said, "Oh, let him go. He's such a baby that he'll probably start crying if he gets caught again."

Brian turned, and ran up onto the deck, and into the house. A few minutes later, he saw the mother come out of the house, and proceed across the yard with Brian in tow.

"Amanda," she said. "Brian said you won't let him play anymore. Is that true?"

"He won't play right, Mom. He didn't find anyone, and he won't be it again."

"Jon said he would be it," Brian complained. "But Amanda still didn't want me to play."

"Well, Amanda," Rachel admonished. "Here's your choice. If Brian can't play, then you can't play either. You decide."

"He can play," Amanda replied sullenly. "But if he gets caught again, he has to be it."

"That's fair," Rachel said. "Okay, Brian?"

"Okay," Brian agreed.

Satisfied, Rachel went back into the house. Jon leaned against the tree, and began counting, as the other children scattered to find a hiding place. When Jon started his search, Brian was caught again, and agreed to be it as he had promised. He closed his eyes, and began counting.

The man watched with interest as, instead of finding a place to hide Amanda motioned for the other boys to come over to the fence, where she was standing. They were close enough for him to easily hear every word.

"Let's play a trick on him," Amanda whispered. "We can go next door, to your house Adam, and watch him try to find us."

"I don't know," Jon said. "That's seems awfully mean."

"It's not mean," insisted Amanda. "It'll be funny."

"Won't he get scared?" Taran asked.

"No," Amanda assured him. "There won't be anything to get scared about. We'll only be gone for a couple of minutes."

The others looked undecided, but they finally agreed.

"Let's hurry up," Amanda said, "He's almost done counting."

He watched as the children ran to the house next door, and disappeared through the door. He watched as Brian began his fruitless, meaningless search. His mind drifted back to that day so many years ago. He remembered how he had searched until well after dark, only to find out later that they had all gone home, and left him there alone. Just as these children had done today. He felt the pain as if it were happening all over again. He remembered how he had cried that night, and then swore to himself that he would never let them make him cry again. He concentrated very hard, and turned the pain he was feeling now, into anger.

He was glad that he had decided to watch and listen, that day. The things that he saw and heard, convinced him that he had to take the risk. Brian was so small, so innocent, and so defenseless. He reminded him more of himself than any of the others had. No matter how difficult it would be, or how afraid he was of her too curious mother, he had to get to Amanda. He had to protect Brian from her.

Chapter 32

Rachel and Sara sat at Rachel's kitchen table, scanning the classified ads. They were trying to find a house on the shore, that they could rent. Michael had readily agreed to them taking the kids to the beach for a week, and Scott hadn't been given a choice. They had even discussed the possibility of the two men going camping together, while the women and kids were away. But, since it was so late in the season, Rachel and Sara were having a problem finding a house to rent.

"Let's face it," Sara said, with disappointment. "We may have to settle for a motel."

"I don't know about you," Rachel said, "But, I don't think I'd *survive* a week in a motel room with my two kids."

"Let's keep looking," Sara agreed.

Just then, they heard a knock at the door, and Christie's familiar voice.

Sara glared at Rachel, and whispered, "You didn't tell me her ankle was better,"

"I didn't think you'd come over here if I did," Rachel whispered back, and then went to the door.

Christie hobbled in, still using her crutches, and immediately launched into a monologue about her trials and tribulations of the past two weeks. Sara listened to her for the first few minutes, and then as her attention wandered, she began scanning the headlines of the newspaper. When she saw the headline, "AUTHORITIES FIND POSSIBLE CONNECTION BETWEEN MISSING CHILDREN", she read the article closely.

"Rachel!" she cried, interrupting Christie in mid sentence, and pointing at the headline. "Did you read this?"

"I didn't even see it. What connection?"

"They said they don't know yet if it means anything, and even though each child is from a different area of New England, they all often played at a playground near their house."

Christie was feeling a little put out that her moment in the spotlight was interrupted. She saw the disturbed look on Rachel's face, and said, "What kind of a connection is that? Most kids play at playgrounds near their houses."

"I guess you're right," Rachel said, turning towards Sara, and giving her a warning look. "They're so desperate to solve these disappearances, that they're probably grasping at straws."

Sara understood Rachel's look immediately, and knew that they would talk more about this later, when Christie wasn't around.

"We have some good news," Rachel said to Christie, changing the subject. "We're going to be renting a place at the beach this summer, for a week."

"I thought Michael hated the beach," Christie replied.

"Oh, Michael's not going," Rachel corrected her, "Sara and I are taking our kids. Michael and Scott will probably go camping somewhere, while we're gone."

"You're taking separate vacations?" Christie asked.

"I guess we are," Rachel said. "I didn't really think about it like that."

"Danny and I would never take separate vacations. We couldn't stand to be away from each other that long," Christie replied, with a hint of superiority in her voice.

"Gag me," Sara mumbled to herself.

Rachel heard Sara's remark, and was afraid Christie might have too, so she said loudly, "Anyway, we're trying to find a place to rent, but we're afraid that we waited too long."

"Why don't you call a realtor," Christie suggested. "Just decide what kind of a place you want to rent, where you want to go, and contact a realtor in that area."

"I *know* it was a good idea," Sara admitted later, after Christie had hobbled home. "It just annoys me that she came up with it."

"I don't care who's idea it was, as long as it works," Rachel laughed, as she picked up the phone and began to dial again. She had finally gotten the name, and telephone number, of a local Realtor on Cape Cod. Sara listened intently as Rachel told the realtor what they were looking for, and what they would be willing to pay. When she hung up the phone, she was smiling.

"She said that they still had a few rental properties available, and since we weren't locked into a certain week, she was sure she'd be able to find something to meet our needs. She's going to get all of the information together, and call me back."

While they waited for the realtor to call, Rachel and Sara began to talk about the newspaper article that they had put off discussing earlier.

"It is sort of creepy," Sara admitted. "You dream about your mother warning you about danger, while you're with her at a playground, and then the only connection they have come up with is that all of these kids spent time at a playground near their houses."

"And don't forget the baseball field. That little Bobby Randolph played Little League Baseball."

Rachel intentionally neglected to remind Sara about the dreams that took place in front of the house on Rocky Ridge, as if not saying it might make it go away.

"Rachel, do you actually believe that your mother is trying to communicate with you? Isn't it more likely that you're dreaming about her because you still miss her so much?"

"I know I still miss her, but my dreams about my mother have always been pleasant, happy dreams. These dreams are scary, and the words she says to me never change. So to answer your question, yes I do believe she's trying to communicate, I just don't know what I'm supposed to do about it."

At that moment, the phone rang, and both women jumped at the sound. Rachel answered it, and silently mouthed "The realtor" to Sara. She wrote down the information that was being given to her, said she would get back to her soon, and hung up the telephone.

"She has three places she thought we'd be interested in," Rachel said, excitedly. "They all have at least three bedrooms, are within walking distance of the beach, and within our price range. They all have an opening in August, too. She gave me the addresses."

"I think we should drive down to the Cape on Saturday, and take a look at them."
Are you serious? Do you really want to drive all the way down there, just for the day?" Rachel asked.
"I'm totally serious," Sara assured her. "How are we ever going to make a decision without seeing what these places look like? It only takes a few hours to get there. We can let the realtor know we're coming down on Saturday, look at the places, make a decision, and give her a check. Maybe she'll even take us around to see them. You don't want to rent something sight unseen, and then find out it's a dump, do you?"
"I guess you're right," Rachel agreed. "But, what about the kids?"
"That's why I suggested going on Saturday. We can leave the kids home with their fathers. That much driving in one day would drive them crazy, not to mention what it would do to *our* sanity."
"Okay, I'll call the realtor, and tell her to expect us on Saturday."
When Rachel made the call, the realtor said that she would be happy to take them around to see the houses, They made plans to meet at the Real Estate office at ten o'clock on Saturday morning.

Chapter 33

Now that he had decided on Amanda, the excitement began to grow. Along with the excitement, however was the frustration of not having a plan. Every other time, he had always known just what he would have to do. Even when the lost puppy had not worked with Bobby, it had not taken him long to devise another plan. After what he had seen during the past week, however, he realized that Amanda was another problem entirely.

He had always been able to observe the others, and learn their routines. They had all spent times away from home without their parents, and sometimes even alone. Amanda was different. He had visited the nearby playground, but never saw her or Brian among the many children playing there. He had driven through the entire neighborhood in the middle of the afternoon, something he had never done before, and discovered where she lived. Only one street away, so close, yet completely out of reach. He hoped he would see her riding her bike around the neighborhood, but the only time he saw her on a bike at all, she was riding up and down her own driveway. She never went to the playground alone, and she didn't ride her bike around the neighborhood, like the other children did. He did see her walk by his house several times, when she was on her way to visit with the people who lived behind him. The only problem was that her mother was always with her.

He had been tempted to give up, but every time he thought about Brian, and the way he had cried when he had discovered that they had left him in the woods, he knew that he had to find a way. He had to protect Brian, and punish her. He imagined what he would do when he finally had her here. He went down to the basement several times, and pretended that she was there. He practiced what he would say to her, and could almost see the fear in her eyes. He had to see that fear for real. He had to know that Brian was safe from her. He had to find a way.

He stood looking out of his front window, wishing she would go by, alone and unprotected. Instead he saw Amanda's mother with her friend on one of their walks. Amanda's mother was wearing something in her hair that looked familiar, a blue and white bow. He ran up to his bedroom, opened his dresser drawer, and took out the yellow and red bow he had found lying on the ground next to his house. Except for the color, it looked exactly like the one Amanda's mother was wearing. Could she have been the one outside of his house that night? It's not possible, he thought. She would have no reason to be there. Even if the bow did belong to her, she probably lost it on one of her many walks past his house, and the wind blew it into his yard. It was just a coincidence that he found it the day after Missy's accident. But he was still glad he had installed the security lights.

He forced the doubts about Amanda's mother from his mind, and again began to concentrate on his problem. He even imagined himself sneaking into Amanda's house in the middle of the night, and snatching her from her bed. He knew that it was a foolishly dangerous idea, but he was getting so desperate, that he actually considered it.

Chapter 34

When Saturday morning arrived, Rachel and Sara were getting ready to head off on their quest to find the perfect house, for their perfect vacation. Scott had decided that, since Sara would be gone for the day, he would take the boys fishing. So her husband and sons were up, and out of the house, before Sara even had her morning coffee.

Since she had plenty of time to get ready, and was anxious to get started, she arrived at Rachel's house a half an hour early. Rachel was in the middle of giving Michael instructions about how to care for Amanda and Brian while she was gone.

"Don't forget to feed them lunch, and I don't mean pop corn and ice cream either," she said to Michael.

"Sounds like a good lunch to me," he laughed. "You have your vegetable, and dairy product, and if I put the ice cream in a cone, that should take care of the bread group, right?"

"Michael!" Rachel cried, in exasperation.

"Take it easy Rachel, I think I can handle this."

"Just make sure you watch them," Rachel warned. "If they want to go to the park, you take them. And they can't ride their bikes out of the driveway, unless you're with them."

"Don't you think you're being a little over protective?" he asked.

"No I don't, and if you don't want to do this, I'll just stay home."

"All right, all right," he said, "No pop corn and ice cream for lunch, and don't let them out of my sight. I've got it, now will you just get going."

Rachel kissed her children goodbye, gave Michael one last warning about his responsibilities, and headed out the door.

As Sara turned the corner, onto the state highway, Rachel said, "I have a really bad feeling about this. Michael just doesn't take anything very seriously."

"I'm sure they'll be fine," Sara assured her. "Even if he does give them junk food for lunch, one meal won't hurt them. We'll be back in plenty of time for dinner."

"I guess you're right. I'm just so used to being the one that always has to take care of them, it's hard to let go."

"Just relax, and try to enjoy the ride. Michael is their father, he won't let anything happen to them."

The drive to Cape Cod was uneventful. The traffic was heavy as they neared the Bourne Bridge, but once they got on to Route 6, it thinned out again. They made good time, and arrived at the Realtor's office ahead of schedule.

The Realtor, a Mrs. Stevens, showed them the listings, and then offered to drive them around to see them. One of the houses was empty, and the owners were staying at another one, so they got to see the inside of both. The third one was rented for the week, and the renters weren't there, so they had to be satisfied to look around the outside. Mrs. Stevens also showed them where the beaches were, within walking distance of all three houses. She pointed out that two were private beaches, but one was a town beach, and had lifeguards on duty seven days a week.

On the ride back to Mrs. Stevens' office, Rachel and Sara discussed the pros and cons of each house, trying to make up their minds. When they arrived at the office, they still had not made a decision. They asked if they could discuss it a while longer, and come back with their decision after lunch. Mrs. Stevens said that she had some paperwork to finish up anyway, and she agreed to meet them back at the office at two o'clock. Rachel and Sara went to a picturesque little restaurant on the bay, and had a leisurely lunch.

Back home, Michael was feeling very proud of himself. He had started the day off right, making sure that the kids had a good, healthy breakfast. He even cleaned up the kitchen, wanting Rachel to find everything as neat as it was when she had left. After breakfast, he took the kids to the park. They played for a while at the playground, and when they got bored with that, he took them down to the duck pond to feed the ducks.

When they got back home, he made macaroni and cheese for them. Not exactly a gourmet meal, but not pop corn and ice cream either. He was feeling quite proud of himself indeed, and had decided that this was easy. He didn't understand why Rachel always got so stressed out. He had just settled down to watch a baseball game on TV, when Amanda asked him if she could go ride her bike.

"Your mother said that you have to stay in the driveway unless I'm with you," he said.

"Then come with me," she answered.

"Aw honey, I'm just about to watch this game. Why don't you watch it with me."

"Please Daddy," she begged. "If you don't want to come outside, can't I just ride up and down the street? I'm almost ten years old. Everyone else my age gets to ride all around the neighborhood, but I'll just stay in front of the house, I promise."

Michael looked at the TV, saw that the game was just starting, and then looked doubtfully back at his daughter.

The trouble was he agreed with her. When he was her age, he was riding his bike all over town.

"You promise you'll stay right in front of the house?" he asked.

"I promise. Don't worry Daddy, I'm a good rider."

"Can I go too?" Brian asked.

"Sorry sport, you're still a little too shaky since I took your training wheels off," Michael replied "Why don't you play with your puzzles for a while."

If this had been Rachel, Brian would have said that he could ride just as good as Amanda could, and he would have whined that it wasn't fair, but he didn't have the nerve to argue with his father. He watched Amanda skip out the door, and went to his room, to play alone.

Amanda wished that her mother would go somewhere every day. Her father was so much more fun to be around, and he didn't treat her like a baby. She rode her bike in and out of the driveway, and up and down the street, for almost an hour. It was starting to get really warm in the sun, and she was sweating. She didn't know that Taran and Joey had gone fishing with their father, and imagined them swimming in their pool. She wished she was there with them. She knew that if she asked her father to bring her over there that he would say that they had to be invited first. Maybe if she rode past their house, they would see her, and ask her to come swimming. She could tell them that she wasn't supposed to be over there alone, but if they gave her time to get home, and then called to invite her maybe her father would bring her over.

Amanda went in the house on the pretense of getting a glass of water, but she really wanted to see what her father was doing. Brian heard her come in, and came running into the kitchen.

"Are you all done riding your bike? Do you want to play a game?" he asked.

Amanda wanted to tell him to get lost, but decided against it. If she made him mad, he might come outside, and stand in the driveway just to bug her. Then she wouldn't be able to ride over to Aunt Sara's house.

"Almost," she answered, sweetly. "I came in to get a drink. I just want to ride for a few more minutes, and then I'll come in and play with you."

"Okay, I'll be in my room setting up the game," he said, as he ran back to his bedroom.

Amanda crept to the doorway of living room, and peaked around the corner. Her father was still absorbed in the baseball game. He didn't even look like he knew that she had come into the house. She crept back through the kitchen, and silently went out the door.

As soon as she was outside, she jumped on her bike, and rode toward Aunt Sara's house. When she got there, she expected to hear Taran, Joey, and their friends in the pool, but everything was quiet. She rode up the driveway, and was surprised to see that the pool was empty. She wondered why they weren't swimming on such a hot day. Then she noticed that

Uncle Scott's boat was gone. They must have gone fishing, she thought.

Disappointed, she got on her bike, and headed back home. She rode slowly along Heritage Drive, in no hurry to get home. As she rode up Sunrise, and then turned the corner onto Rocky Ridge, she wondered if her father had noticed that she was gone. She hoped not, she would be in real trouble if he had. She started to pedal faster. It was hard because the road here was rocky, and rutted. She also tried to avoid the numerous puddles caused by the rain the night before. Maybe her father would set up the sprinkler, in the back yard. It wasn't the same as a swimming pool, but at least she could cool off, and not have to play that stupid game with Brian.

Chapter 35

He was standing at his living room window, looking out at the street, and feeling like a complete failure. It had been a week since he had decided on Amanda, and he still did not have a plan. He had tortured himself every day thinking about what she must be doing to Brian, how much the poor little boy must be suffering, but he still had no idea what to do about it.

As he stood there, he saw her go riding by on her bike. *I must be imagining it,* he thought. *Have I been thinking about her so much, that I'm starting to see things? If it really was Amanda, her mother should be coming along right behind her.* He waited a few minutes, and when he didn't see her mother, he ran up the stairs. He looked out of his bedroom window, and realized that he didn't imagine it. There she was. She was standing in the driveway of the house behind him, staring into the back yard. He noticed that both the car and truck, that were usually parked there, were gone. *There's no one home,* he thought. *She must have gone there to visit, but no one is home.*

He saw her get on her bike, and begin to pedal slowly down the driveway toward the street. *This might be his chance, his only chance.* He yanked open the dresser drawer, and grabbed the bottle of chloroform. As he ran out of the bedroom door, he snatched a shirt that was lying on the bed, and twisted the cap off the bottle. He poured the chloroform on the shirt, as he ran down the stairs. The liquid spilled all over the stairs, but he didn't notice or care. He stopped long enough to take a log, from next to the fireplace, before he bolted out of the front door.

As he got into his front yard, he slowed to a fast walk, just in case anyone was walking by. Not that it would have mattered. He was sweating so profusely, and had such a wild look about him, that if anyone had seen him they would have known something was wrong. As luck would have it, there was no one in sight. He walked quickly down to the bushes growing along the edge of the road, and peered around them towards the end of the street. She was coming! He was so afraid that he had missed her, but she was coming.

He looked up and down the street, and was glad to see that, except for Amanda, it was empty. He would have a real problem if someone unexpectedly turned the corner, but he had to do it, it would probably be his only chance.

He crouched down, at the end of the row of bushes, with the log in one hand, and the chloroform soaked shirt in the other. Amanda was pedaling faster now, and because of the rough road, she was already having trouble keeping her balance. When she was almost to the end of the bushes, he threw the log out in front of her. When her front wheel hit the log, the wheel turned, twisting the handlebars out of her hands. The bike fell to the side, taking Amanda down with it, and landing on top of her. There was still no one on the street, so he rushed out from behind the bushes.

"Are you all right?" he asked, as he knelt down next to her. Before she had a chance to answer he pushed the shirt, still clutched in his hand, over her face. She struggled for a few seconds, trying to get the offensive thing off of her, and then she was still.

He threw the bike off of her, scooped her up in his arms, and ran into the house. He stood inside his front door for a minute, trying to catch his breath, and then brought her down to the basement. After securely locking her in the special room, he went back to the living room, and stood there looking out of the window.

He still didn't see anyone, and started to breathe easier. Since there were no other houses on this part of Rocky Ridge, he knew that no one could have seen him from inside their house. He had done it, he couldn't believe that he had done it. She was here, Brian was safe, and no one would ever know.

Suddenly, the sight of Amanda's bike lying in the road in front of his house, hit him. Every other time, it had not mattered if he left their bikes where they were, but this time was different. This time the bike was right there in front of his own house. He had to get it. He went out the front door, and walked cautiously down to the road. There was still no one around, so he picked up the bike, and wheeled it to the back of the house. He didn't want to take the chance of leaving it outside, so he brought it down to the basement, and stashed it behind the furnace.

As he had wheeled the bike around the corner of the house, he noticed the security light with the missing bulb. He went back outside now, and using a stepladder, replaced the bulb. He had a reason to want all of the lights working now. He had a reason for getting up in the morning. He had a reason for living. He had Amanda!

Chapter 36

Rachel and Sara finished their lunch, and drove back to the Real Estate office. They had finally decided on the house in Dennis. It was a little more expensive then the others, but it had four bedrooms, so they would have enough room if the kids wanted to bring friends along. Rachel and Sara could share a room, and Brian could even bunk with them on a cot, if it was necessary. The thing that really swayed the decision though, was the beach. This house had the town beach, and both of the women felt better knowing that there would be lifeguards on duty. They gave Mrs. Stevens a check for the down payment, and agreed to send the balance two weeks before the start of their vacation.

On the drive home, they talked about how much fun it would be spending the week together, and how they hoped it wouldn't rain. They had been tempted to stop at some of the quaint gift shops along Route 6A, but it was already going on three o'clock, and Rachel was anxious to get home.

"I know it's probably ridiculous," she said. "But I just don't feel comfortable leaving the kids alone with Michael for this long."

Sara had said that she understood, as she wistfully looked at the shops they passed. Oh well, we'll have plenty of time to shop when we come down in August, she thought.

They ran into much more traffic on the way home, and it took over three hours to get back. Rachel seemed to grow more anxious, and apologized several times saying, "I don't know what's wrong with me."

When they turned onto Rollins Avenue, it was Rachel who first noticed the police cruiser parked in her driveway.

"Oh my God!" she screamed.

Sara pulled in the driveway behind the cruiser. She had barely stopped the car, when Rachel flung the door open, and raced into the house. Scott, Taran,

144

and Joey were sitting on the front steps, looking very
upset, and Sara rushed over to them.

"What's wrong?" she asked, apprehensively.

"Amanda is missing," Scott answered, and when he
looked up at Sara, she could see the fear on his face.

"Missing? What do you mean missing? Missing from
where? For how long?"

"According to Michael, she went outside to ride her
bike at around two o'clock. About an hour later, he
went out to check on her, and couldn't find her. He
called all of her friends, and none of them had seen
her. We got home around four o'clock, and helped him
search the whole neighborhood. I finally convinced
him to call the police about a half hour ago."

"Two o'clock," Sara repeated. "It's after six now.
You mean no one has seen her for over four hours?"

"Mom, has something bad happened to Amanda?" Joey
asked, his voice quivering.

"No, of course not," Sara answered, as she pulled
her son close to her. "She's fine, she has to be."

"Oh no," Sara suddenly cried. "Did you check the
pool?"

"That's the first place I looked," Scott said. "I
know how much she loves to swim, and it was pretty hot
today. She wasn't in the pool."

"Thank God," Sara said, but a feeling of dread had
already begun to descend on her. Amanda would never
have gone very far away by herself, she thought. And
if she was close by, they would have found her by now.

"I'd better go check on Rachel," she said to Scott,
"She must be going out of her mind. Why don't you
take the boys home."

"Okay, but call me if you find out anything."

As Sara hugged each of her sons tightly, she told
them not to worry, and that everything would be all
right. She only wished that she believed it.

Rachel found Michael sitting in the living room,
with Brian on his lap, talking to a police officer.
She rushed over, and scooped Brian into her arms.

"Thank God you're all right," she said "I thought
something terrible had happened to you."

"I'm okay Mommy," Brian said. "But, Amanda ran away."

Rachel immediately felt guilty, and embarrassed. What was wrong with her? A police officer was sitting in her living room, and as soon as she had seen that Brian was all right, she hadn't even cared why he was there. She hadn't even asked where Amanda was. Now the officer, and Michael were both looking at her, waiting for her reaction. She looked at Michael for the first time, and realized that he had been crying.

"What does he mean 'Amanda ran away'?" she asked.

"Brian, why don't you go play in your room for a while," Michael said "The policeman and I have to talk to Mommy for a while."

Brian was about to object, but when he saw the look on his father's face, he quickly went to his room.

After Brian had left the room, Michael turned to Rachel, and said, "We don't know what happened to her, she's just gone. I haven't seen her since two o'clock, and I don't know where she is," then he started to cry.

Rachel looked from Michael to the police officer, trying to let the words penetrate her brain. Did he say she was gone? No, she must have misunderstood him. Why was he crying? And, why was this policeman looking at her like that? Like he felt sorry for her. All of a sudden, everything started to get blurry, and the room started to turn white. Michael jumped up, and tried to catch her as she fainted.

When Sara came into the house, she found Rachel lying on the couch, and Michael wiping a cold cloth across her face.

"What happened," Sara asked, as she quickly crossed the room, and knelt down beside her friend.

"She fainted," Michael said. "I told her that Amanda was missing, and she just fainted."

"Rachel," Sara said, gently. "Rachel, are you all right?"

Rachel opened her eyes, and saw Michael and Sara next to her. At first she thought it had been a nightmare, but then she saw the policeman standing a short distance away, and she knew it was real. Her daughter was really missing.

Sara had expected Rachel to be hysterical. She knew she would have been if one of her children was missing, but Rachel's strength had amazed her. After she had fully regained consciousness, she had assured everyone that she was all right, and she didn't need a doctor. She had given the officer a recent picture of Amanda, and had thanked him when he said that every officer in town would have a copy of the picture, and be on the look out for her. Sara had wanted to ask him if that was all they were going to do, but she didn't want to take the chance of upsetting Rachel.

Rachel seemed to be almost *too* much in control, and Sara thought that she might snap at any minute. Even though Michael said he had already called Amanda's friends, Rachel called them all again. She asked them to let her know immediately if they saw her, or heard from her. She also insisted on searching the neighborhood herself. Michael tried to tell her that he had already done that, but it was as if she couldn't even hear him. She said that she knew Amanda was close by, and she was probably just afraid to come home.

Sara took Michael aside and said, "I think she just has to feel like she's doing something. I know you need her to help you through this, Michael, but if she has to sit here waiting, I think she'll crumble. You stay here with Brian, in case someone calls, and I'll go with her."

As Sara started to follow Rachel out the door, Rachel turned to Michael, and said, "Aren't you coming with me? Don't you even want to look for her?"

"Rachel, I told you I already..." Michael began, but Sara interrupted him.

"Rachel, Michael has to stay here with Brian. You can't leave him here alone, and someone should be here in case someone calls with some news."

"Oh, of course," Rachel said. "Someone has to stay here." But, she looked at both Michael and Sara as if she didn't really understand.

When the two women got outside, Rachel began to walk quickly down the driveway.

"Rachel," Sara called out. "Don't you want to take my car? We can go a lot faster that way."

When Rachel hesitated, looking uncertain, Sara hurried to reach her and gently steered her toward the car.

As Sara backed out of the driveway, Rachel said, "It's my fault you know."

"What's your fault?" Sara asked.

"That she's gone."

"Of course it's not your fault," Sara assured her. "It isn't anyone's fault."

"Then why did she run away?"

Sara wanted to assure Rachel that Amanda didn't run away. That she would never have done that. But, as she opened her mouth, the reality of what she was about to say hit her. If she didn't run away, where was she? The alternative was too horrible to think about, so she helplessly said, "I don't know."

As Sara drove up and down the streets of Eden Park, she slowed in front of each house, and they looked up the driveways. They didn't really think they would find her, because her friends didn't live near here, and the only other kids in the neighborhood that she knew well, were Taran and Joey. But, they still searched every street, and every house, hoping against hope that somehow she would appear. It was starting to get dark, and Sara suggested that they go back to Rachel's to see if Michael had heard anything. Rachel reluctantly agreed, but she asked Sara to drive around, just one more time.

They drove around the neighborhood again, still without any success. As Sara began to drive back to Rachel's house, Rachel began to cry. Sara pulled the car over to the side of the road, and hugged her friend.

"Sara," Rachel managed to say between sobs. "I can't fool myself anymore. She didn't run away, and we both know it."

Sara hugged Rachel tighter as tears began to fall from her own eyes.

"You can't give up hope, Rachel. You have to believe she's okay, and she'll be back home again."

"Like all of those other kids?" Rachel asked, miserably "Sara, I'm so scared. What if something terrible has happened to her, and I never see her again?"

Sara wanted to be able to tell Rachel that they would find Amanda, and that it wasn't the same as those other missing children, but she couldn't say it. She had always been honest with Rachel, and as much as she wanted to make her feel better at this moment, the lie wouldn't come. It felt so inadequate, but all she could say was, "We won't give up, Rachel. We won't give up until we find her."

Rachel looked at Sara, and saw the same pain in her eyes, that she was feeling herself.

"I'm going to walk home from here," she said. "I'll meet you back at my house."

"Rachel, please come back with me."

"Don't worry, I'll be there in a few minutes. I just need some time alone."

Sara knew it would do no good to argue with her.

"Don't be too long," she said. "Michael and Brian both need you."

Chapter 37

He sat in the dark, staring into space. It had been hours since he had taken Amanda, and he was still shaking. At first he had felt excited. He couldn't believe his good fortune to have been at the right place, and at the right time. He had felt like it was fate that had provided the opportunity for him to succeed. Then he started to realize all of the things that could have gone wrong. Even though his house was the only one on this part of Rocky Ridge, it was not in a remote or deserted area. People were always walking and driving by. Someone could have come upon him at any time. Someone could have seen Amanda's bike lying in front of his house. Maybe someone had! He started to worry that, at any moment, the police would be at his door demanding to search his house. That was when he had begun to shake uncontrollably.

Now, hours later, he was still unable to control his fear. It was like waiting for a disaster, that you had no control over, to strike. Even after he had taken Bobby, when he had been afraid that someone had seen him, it was not like this. This was so much worse. He didn't even feel safe in his own house, and he had always felt safe here before.

With all of the others, he had been anxious to go down to them, and get started. He couldn't wait for them to wake up. But now, even though he was sure that Amanda was awake, he couldn't make himself go down there. He couldn't face her while he was feeling so afraid himself. So he sat there, waiting for fate to take it's course. Either the police would be at his door, or eventually the fear would go away, and he would feel confident and powerful again. In a way, it would be a turning point. If he was caught, it would be all over. If he wasn't, it proved that his mission was just, and he should continue. Either way, he was ready to accept it.

When Amanda woke up, the first thing that she was aware of, was that her leg hurt. It was scraped and

150

bruised, where the bike had fallen on her, and she cried out when she moved it. Slowly, she became aware of her surroundings. The light filtering in around the edge of the window near the ceiling, was just enough for her to make out the sparse furnishings in the room. She could tell it was a cellar, and she knew just what cellar it was. The spooky looking house on Rocky Ridge.

She had fallen in front of that house, and a man had run out from behind the bushes. He had asked if she was all right, and then pushed that smelly cloth over her face. She didn't know how she knew he had brought her into the house, she just did. She also didn't know why he had done that, but she knew it couldn't be good, and she had to get out of here. She knew that she was going to be in a lot of trouble when she got home, but she didn't care. She sensed that she would be in a lot more trouble if she stayed here.

The shaking had finally stopped. He was beginning to feel less afraid, but he still didn't feel completely safe. He considered going down, and checking on her, but didn't want her to see him this way. He had to see the fear in her, and he couldn't let her see the fear in him first. He decided to go to bed, and see what the morning would bring. If no one had come here looking for her by then, he would know that he was safe.

As he was lying in his bed, and trying to make himself sleep, he wondered again why he taken such a chance. Why had he rushed out there, and done what he had done. He had just reacted to the situation, and not really thought about anything else. It was a foolish, and dangerous thing to do. Why had he done it? When he thought about Brian, he knew why. He had to protect him from Amanda, no matter what the risk.

A line from the Bible, that his mother used to read when he was a little boy, came back to him. "His children are far from safety. They shall be crushed at the gate without a rescuer." He didn't know where in the Bible it was from. He didn't even know what it was supposed to mean, but he knew what it meant to him. *It didn't matter what happened to him, as long as Brian was safe. If they came looking for her, he would make sure that she was not rescued.*

Amanda had been awake most of the night, trying to find a way out. She had found the switch on the wall, and turned the light on. It was still dirty and creepy in there, but not half as scary. She had pulled the chair over to the wall, and standing on it, had tried to reach the window. The window itself was way too high, but when she stood on her tiptoes she could just about reach the heavy cloth that covered it. She pulled at it with the tips of her fingers, until it ripped enough for her to get a good hold on it.

Then she yanked at it with all of her might, until a piece of it ripped away, uncovering part of the window. She could see that it was dark outside. Her mother was probably home by now, and really mad at her. I'd still rather be there, she thought.

She went over to the switch on the wall. It was higher than the switches in her house, and she had to stretch her arm up to reach it. She started turning it on and off. She knew that this house was usually dark at night. Maybe someone would see the light going on and off, and come and find her. She stood there turning the light on and off, until she couldn't hold her arm up any longer. Then, she tried pulling on the door again, but it wouldn't move. She sat down on the dirty mattress, discouraged, and tried to think of something else to do. She didn't want to sleep, but exhaustion soon overcame her. She drifted off to sleep, imagining her father breaking down the door, and taking her home.

Chapter 38

Rachel got out of the car, and watched as Sara drove away. She walked home slowly, with her head down, pausing along the way to look between the houses. Although she knew it was unrealistic, she still hoped that she would see her daughter there. She thought about all of the times she had yelled at Amanda, and called her hateful names. Had she really called her a 'mean little witch'? The guilt she was feeling now was so overwhelming, that she didn't think she could stand it. If only she had her back again, she would make it all up to her.

When she walked by the house on Rocky Ridge, she shivered as the now familiar chill went down her spine. She stopped, stared at the house in the fading light, and the dreams she had been having hit her like a tidal wave. She was standing in front of this house with her mother, and her mother was saying, "Be careful Rachel. Your family is in danger. You have to stop him, before it's too late."

She stood there, looking at the house, but not really seeing it. As the light faded, a feeling of certainty came over her. Amanda was in there. She could feel it. She didn't know what to do, but she knew she had to do something soon. Would Sara help her, or would she try to stop her? She remembered the pain, and the look of helplessness on Sara's face. She'll help me, she decided. She'll help me tonight. She forced herself to walk away from the house, and hurried the rest of the way home. When she got there, Sara and Michael were sitting at the kitchen table, and Brian was in the living room, watching cartoons.

"Are you all right?" Michael asked, as she sat down at the table.

"Have you heard anything?" she asked, ignoring his question.

"No, a few people have called, asking if they can do anything, but no one has seen her."

Hearing his mother's voice, Brian came running into the kitchen, and Michael immediately told him to go back, and watch his cartoons. Rachel gave her husband a look as cold as ice, as she pulled Brian onto her lap, and hugged him tightly.

"When is Amanda coming home?" Brian asked.

Rachel bit her lip, trying to hold back the tears, "Soon honey, she'll be home soon," she said.

"She promised she would stay right in front of the house, and that she would play a game with me when she was done riding her bike." Brian said, innocently.

Rachel looked at Michael, and saw the look of apprehension on his face. Still staring at Michael, she put Brian down, and said, "Why don't you finish watching your cartoons, and I'll read you a story before bedtime."

After Brian had left the room, she calmly said to Michael, "She was riding her bike? You let her ride her bike on the street alone?"

"She said she would stay right in front of the house. I didn't think it was any big deal. When I was her age, I rode my bike all over town."

"And I'm always so over protective, right? Didn't you even think about the fact that two of those missing kids were riding their bikes when they disappeared, and one of them was right in front of her own house?" she asked, coldly.

"Rachel, I'm sorry."

"You're sorry? Oh, you're sorry. Our daughter is gone, but you're sorry, so that makes everything all right."

"Rachel don't..." Michael began.

"Don't what?" Rachel interrupted. "Don't make you face the fact that if you had been watching her, like I asked you to, she would still be here?"

When Rachel saw the stricken look on Michael's face, she knew that she shouldn't have said what she did, but she couldn't stop the words from tumbling out of her mouth. The truth was, that she was feeling so guilty herself, it was easier to blame her husband for Amanda's disappearance.

"I'm sorry," she said, as she stood up, and put her arms around her husband. "I know it's not your fault, I don't even know why I said that."

"But you're right," Michael said, as the tears flowed silently down his face. "If I had been watching her, this never would have happened."

Rachel and Michael stood there for a few minutes, clinging to each other, and not saying anything. Sara felt her tears choking her, as she watched them. When they finally let go of each other, Rachel asked,

"Where did you find her bike?"

"We didn't," Michael answered. "Her bike is gone too."

Rachel looked first surprised, then thoughtful, and then she said, "Michael will you read Brian a story? I have to talk to Sara for a while."

After Michael had left the room, Sara said, "Maybe it isn't the same person. When the other kids disappeared, they found their bikes."

"I know," Rachel said. "And I think I know why Amanda's bike is missing. He couldn't leave it where someone might find it."

"What are you talking about? Who couldn't?"

"I think she decided, since I wasn't here to stop her, to ride her bike around the neighborhood. And, when she rode by his house, he grabbed her. He couldn't leave her bike in front of his house, so he took that too."

"Rachel, are you talking about the house on Rocky Ridge?"

"Of course I am," Rachel said, impatiently.

Sara didn't like the look in Rachel eyes. It was almost maniacal.

"Don't look at me like that, Sara, I'm not crazy. It all fits. Look at the dreams I've been having. In a playground, all the missing kids played at a playground near their houses. In a ball field, Bobby Randolph played baseball. In front of the house on Rocky Ridge...My mother warning me that my family was in danger, and that I had to stop him before it was too late."

Sara looked at Rachel skeptically. She knew that her need to find Amanda, coupled with her obsession about the house on Rocky Ridge, would make the scenario she had just outlined seem perfectly logical. How would she ever convince her that it just was not possible.

"Are you going to call the police?"

"No, not yet. I can tell by the look on your face, that you think I'm being totally irrational. How can I hope to convince them, if I can't even convince you."

"Then what are you going to do?"

"I want to go there tonight, and look around."

"Rachel, you can't!"

"I have to Sara. When I was walking home, I stood in front of that house, and I felt that she was in there. If she is, I have to find her before it's too late."

"But you won't be able to see anything at night. As soon as you get close to the house, those motion detector lights will come on. What will you do then."

"I forgot about the lights," Rachel said, miserably.

"Rachel, let's wait until the morning. We can walk by, and look for any sign that Amanda has been by there. Then at least the police will have a reason to knock on the door, and ask whoever lives there, if they have seen her."

"I guess you're right. If she is there, I don't want to spook him into doing anything before I can get to her."

"Good, then you'll wait until tomorrow. Call me as soon as you're ready to go. And, promise me you won't do anything tonight."

"I promise, and thanks Sara. I know you think I'm crazy, but at least you're willing to go along with me."

Up to a point Rachel, Sara thought, only up to a point.

Brian was asleep, and Rachel and Michael sat in front of the TV, looking at it but not really seeing it. They had tried to talk about Amanda, and what they could do to find her, but the more they talked, the more hopeless it seemed, until they both fell silent.

Sometime after midnight, Michael had fallen asleep, and Rachel was too restless to sit any longer. After checking on Brian again, she left the house and began to walk aimlessly, until she found herself in front of the house on Rocky Ridge. She walked slowly back and forth in front of the house, looking for any sign of movement. Since she could see the shadow of the van parked toward the back, she knew that someone was there, but the house was completely dark. When she walked by the house again, she thought she saw a flicker of light coming from somewhere in the back. There it was again, like a dim light going on and off. She had promised Sara that she would wait until the morning to come here, but she had to find out where that light was coming from.

She walked slowly up the side of the front yard, trying to keep as far away from the house as she could. She managed to get by the light at the front corner of the house, without activating the motion detector. The yard narrowed toward the back, and as she inched along the fence, and was almost even with the back of the house, the light on the back corner of the house went on. She froze where she was, caught in the glare of the light, and sure that the dogs would start barking at any minute.

She was surprised when she didn't hear anything, and hurried back to the street to crouch behind the bushes. The same bushes that she had hidden behind with Sara and Jenna, what seemed like a lifetime ago. She waited a few minutes, and the light on the house went out. She stayed there for a while longer, waiting to see the flickering light she had seen before, but the house remained dark. Reluctantly, she walked back to her house, made a pot of coffee, and waited for the sun to come up.

Chapter 39

He woke up with a start, unable to remember at first why he should be afraid. The sun was just starting to come up, and he looked around the dimly lit room. He was in his own bed. They hadn't come looking for her all night, which probably meant that he was safe. He felt as if a great weight had been lifted from his chest, and was anxious to see Amanda. She had probably been awake all night, crying, and feeling scared. He would probably see the fear on her face as soon as he opened the door.

When he walked into the room, he was puzzled to see that the light was on. He didn't even remember turning it on when he brought her in here yesterday, but he had been so shaken, it didn't surprise him. He was surprised, however, that she was asleep. He had pictured her crouched in a corner, trembling with fear. He noticed the chair over by the window, and smiled to himself. They all tried that. His gaze wandered up the wall to the window, that was always too high, and he saw the sunlight streaming through the partially uncovered pane.

"WHAT DID YOU DO?" he screamed, as he raced across the room.

When he reached the other side of the room, he climbed onto the chair, and frantically stuffed the dangling piece of cloth around the edge of the window, until it was covered again.

When he had screamed, Amanda was jolted awake. She started to sit up, and then pushed herself back against the wall, as he ran across the room. She thought he was coming for her, and was surprised when he ran past her to the window. She relaxed a little when he started covering the window, and watched him curiously. He looked like he was more afraid than she was. When he had finished, he got down from the chair, turned to Amanda, and said, "What did you think you were doing?"

Amanda knew that it would be dangerous for her if he knew that she had been trying to signal someone last night. Especially if he thought she had succeeded.

"It was dark in here, and I was scared. I wanted to let some light in."

"Don't lie to me." he said, menacingly "The light was on, it wasn't dark in here."

I found the light switch after I pulled the curtain off the window. That's when I turned the light on."

"You think you're really smart don't you?" he asked.

Amanda wanted to say "yes", but she could tell by the way he had asked the question that it would make him mad. She wasn't sure how to answer him, so she didn't say anything.

"What's the matter?" he sneered. "Don't you have anything to say?"

"Who are you, and why did you bring me here?" she asked.

"I am a protector, and a punisher." he proclaimed proudly.

"What are you talking about?" she asked.

"They all play dumb like that," he said, more to himself than to her. "But they understand, they all understand."

"Understand what? The only thing I understand is that you'd better let me out of here."

"I don't think that would be a good idea. You have to be here, so that Brian can be protected."

"Brian? My brother Brian? He doesn't even know you, and he sure doesn't need you to protect him from anything."

"Oh, but he does, he needs me to protect him from you. You are a cruel child, Amanda, and cruel children should be punished."

He waited expectantly for the look of fear to fill her eyes, and was puzzled, when he didn't see it.

"You're crazy," she said. "And you're the one that's going to need protection, when my mother and father find out what you did."

Susan Biscoe

She saw a look she didn't quite understand cross his face when she mentioned her mother and father. It wasn't quite fear, but something close to it. It was only there for a second, before he shook it off, and said, "What makes you think your mother will even care? How do you know that your mother isn't the one who told me to punish you?"

"Because my mother does just fine punishing me all by herself," Amanda said, bitterly.

"Well maybe she needs help this time. Maybe she needs help punishing the 'MEAN LITTLE WITCH'"

Amanda's mouth dropped open, and her eyes widened. How did he know her mother had called her that? Did she really tell him about her? Did she really tell him to punish her? And did her father know?

It wasn't exactly the reaction he was looking for. It was more shock than fear, but at least it was something. He was going to say more, but decided that this would be a good time to leave her alone, and let her think about it. He turned, and left the room, and this time he took the chair with him.

Chapter 40

When daylight finally arrived, Rachel turned on the TV in the kitchen, and turned down the volume, so it wouldn't wake Michael or Brian. Michael had fallen asleep on the couch, and she had covered him with a blanket, rather than waking him up. The local news was on, and they were showing a picture of Amanda. The same picture Rachel had given to the police officer the night before. Her daughter's face filled the screen, and Rachel choked back the sobs that immediately tightened her throat. Then, Amanda's picture shrunk to the upper corner of the screen, and the pictures of four other children appeared below it. Rachel recognized Missy's picture immediately, and knew that these must be the other missing children. It had all seemed so unreal, that several times during the night she had gone to Amanda's room, expecting to see her asleep in her bed. How could this be happening? Why was it happening?

As Rachel reached to turn up the sound on the TV, the telephone rang, it's piercing sound breaking the stillness in the house. Before she could reach the phone on the wall, Michael picked up the one in the living room. She could hear him talking to someone. She thought it was probably Sara, when to her surprise, Sara came in the back door.

Sara was about to ask Rachel how she was doing, when Michael walked into the kitchen, brushing his hair back from his face with both hands.

"Who was that on the phone?" Rachel asked, hopefully.

"It was the police," seeing the look on his wife's face, Michael held up both hands, and answered her unasked question.

"No, they didn't find anything. They just wanted to let us know that they're going to start dragging Eden Pond."

"Dragging the pond? For what? OH NO!" Rachel wailed. "No Michael, they don't think that she's there? Why would they think that? Did they find something? Did they find her bike there?"

"No, they didn't find anything there. When a child is missing, and there's a body of water nearby, they have to check it out. It's just routine, Rachel, that's why they called. They wanted to let us know, so we wouldn't jump to any conclusions."

Michael walked over and put his arms around his wife. Rachel's shoulders shook convulsively, as she sobbed into his chest.

Sara stood in the doorway, close to tears herself. Watching her friend go through this was the most painful thing she had ever done in her life. She wanted to say something, but she felt like she would be intruding on Michael and Rachel. She started to back out the door, when Rachel turned, and said, "Sara, please don't go. I want you to stay."

Sara sat down at the table, took both of Rachel's hands in her own, and said, "She's not in Eden Pond, Rachel. Amanda would never go near there. You know how she feels about snakes, and that place is literally crawling with them."

"I know," Rachel said, gaining control of herself, "Just the thought of them dragging the pond looking for her, and seeing her picture on TV with all of those other kids..."

"I'm so sorry, Rachel. I wish there was something I could do."

"Will you still come with me, to look around that house."

"You mean on the road, in front of it, right?"

"Yes, for now."

Sara was about to ask her what she meant, and decided not to. She didn't really want to know. Rachel went into the living room, and told Michael that she was going out to get some air, and would be back in a few minutes. Michael knew his wife well enough to know that she had something specific on her mind, but he also knew her well enough to know that she wouldn't share it with him until she was ready.

On the walk over to Rocky Ridge, Rachel confessed
to Sara that she had gone over there around midnight,
the night before. She told her about seeing the light
going on and off in the back of the house, and how she
had tried to investigate.

"Rachel, you promised you wouldn't do that again."
Sara said, with alarm.

"I know I did, and I really didn't plan to, but it
was so strange that I had to try to find out what it
was."

"And did you find out anything?"

"No, when the light on the back corner of the house
came on, I got out of there."

They had almost reached the house, and they began
to walk more slowly. Sara noticed a piece of wood, in
the middle of the road up ahead. Rachel went over,
and picked it up.

"I wonder how it got here," she said.

"Could it have come off one of the oak trees?"

"No, look. It didn't break off, it was sawed off.
It's smooth on both ends, like a piece of firewood."

"Maybe someone had some wood delivered, and it fell
off of a truck."

"At this time of year?"

"No, I guess not."

The two women started walking again, when Rachel
stopped abruptly, and turned around.

"What's wrong?" Sara asked.

"These are bicycle tracks."

"Where?"

"Right here, look."

"But Rachel, kids ride their bikes by here all the
time."

Rachel walked a few more feet, and then looked up
towards the house. She looked back at Sara, and
asked, "And do kids ride their bikes up to that
house?"

"What?"

"Look, the bicycle tracks go from the road, right
across the front yard."

Sara looked where Rachel was pointing, and couldn't
believe what she saw. Rachel was right. The tracks

went right across the front yard, to the back of the house.

"The dirt is dry now, but those tracks were made when it was muddy," Rachel said.

"And the only time it has rained in the past three weeks, was the night before last," Sara said.

They both stood there, staring at the house.

"She's in there," Rachel said, "I know she is."

"I believe you," Sara said, "But, what do we do now?"

Chapter 41

After he had gone, Amanda sat for a long time staring at the door. She knew that as mad as her mother got sometimes, that she would never have told this man to kidnap her. Besides, her mother couldn't have known that she would be riding her bike past this house. It had just been such a shock when he had said it, that she didn't know what to think at first. Now, she was trying to remember when her mother had said that to her. Was it at home, when her friend was sleeping over, and she wouldn't let Brian in her room? Or was it at the park, when she didn't want to push him on the merry-go-round? Wait a minute. Now she remembered. It was in Aunt Sara's pool, when Brian said that she had tried to drown him. As far as she could remember, that was the only time her mother had used those words, and this house was right behind Aunt Sara's house. He must have heard her mother that day. She had yelled so loud that even her father had heard it, and he was inside the house. She felt better. She could admit to herself now that she had wondered, even if it was just for a minute, whether her mother could really hate her enough to want this to happen to her. Now she was sure that he had lied, and she was just as sure that he really was crazy.

Amanda tried to remember what he had said about Brian. It had something to do with protecting him from her. The way he talked about Brian was creepy. Like he knew him, or something. But he couldn't know him, Amanda had never even seen this guy until today. She didn't understand what was going on, but she knew that her mother or father would find her soon. They had to know she was here, her bike was right out there in the road, wasn't it? Then why didn't they come and get her?

He was confused by the way Amanda had acted. She should have been afraid. All of the others had been afraid, especially when he had told them that they should be punished. When he had told her that he was a punisher, she hadn't been scared at all. The only time she had any reaction, was when he had called her a 'mean little witch'. She had really believed that her mother had told him that. He could tell by the look on her face. But, it wasn't enough. He needed to see the fear. He had pictured it so many times, he knew exactly what it would look like. The fear first, then the suffering, then the elimination. He couldn't proceed with the second, until he had achieved the first. He had to see the fear, and he had to see it soon.

He left her alone for several hours, hoping that the solitude would make her more frightened. He went back down the stairs, determined to see the fear in her eyes. When he walked into the room, she looked up at him with her eyes blazing, and said, "I know who you are, you know."

The statement took him by surprise, and he stiffened without realizing why.

"I told you who I am," he said, trying not to betray the uneasiness he felt. "I am a protector, and a punisher."

"You're the man who lives behind my Aunt Sara's house, and I know how you knew what my mother said to me. She never told you to punish me. You were listening to us when we were at Aunt Sara's house. You're nothing but a liar."

"I think you are probably the cruelest child that I've ever seen," he said, sadly. "Brian is not the only one who needs protection from you. I think the whole world needs protection from you."

"You really are crazy aren't you? My mother and father are going to come and get me, and they'll probably bring a whole army of police with them. They'll probably shoot you dead, and I'll be glad."

This was going badly. She wasn't afraid of him at all. The others had all been first confused, then curious, and then afraid. She hadn't been any of those things, and instead of the power he had always felt, he now felt like he was losing control of the whole situation. He had to think, and he couldn't do that with her glaring at him like that.

He left the room quickly, locked the door securely, and hurried up the stairs. He had to get out of there for a while. His ears were still ringing from her words, and he couldn't get them out of his head. He decided to go to the park. He always felt calm there, and he would be able to think. Maybe when he got back, he would have the control again, or maybe he would just have to get rid of her. Having her fear him, and suffer would be good, but the important thing was protecting Brian. And he could only be sure that Brian was safe when she had been eliminated.

Chapter 42

The two women stood silently, looking at the house for a long time, until Rachel finally said, "We have to get in there."

"No," Sara objected, "We have to call the police."

"Sara, I've watched enough real trials on TV to know that the police will not be able to get a search warrant based on bicycle tracks across the front yard. The most they will be able to do is knock on the door, and ask if he's seen her. Who knows what he'll do then. He might panic. We have to get in there first."

"But, how? You've tried twice, and you haven't even been able to get close to the house. How are we going to actually get inside?"

"We know that when the van isn't there, he must be gone. We'll have to watch, and wait for that, and hope that there's only one person living there. I know that she's in there Sara, and she's alive, I can feel it. But, we can't wait too long, I know that too."

Sara wanted to make some kind of argument against what Rachel was planning, but she couldn't think of any. She was right about the police. They wouldn't be able to do anything. Besides, they would probably think it was the ravings of a distraught mother, who was grasping at straws. And, maybe it was. Rachel did have a wild imagination, and she had been obsessed about this house for months, but Sara couldn't shake the feeling that she was right. That Amanda was in there. And, if it turned out that she was there, and Sara didn't help Rachel, she would never be able to live with herself.

"We'd better get out of here now," Sara said. "We don't want him, or whoever it is, to see us standing here."

"You're right. Let's go to your house, and see if there is someplace from there, that we can watch for the van to leave."

They walked quickly to Sara's house. Rachel called Michael as soon as they got there, and told him that she would be at Sara's for a while. She asked him to call her if he heard anything. Michael tried to talk Rachel into coming home, but she said that being at home just made her feel worse. He eventually gave up, and promised to call if he heard anything.

Sara was glad that, although it was Sunday, Scott had gone to work to finish up some paperwork. The boys were still asleep, so she didn't have to try to explain what they were doing. They went up the stairs quietly, and looked out of Sara's bedroom windows. They could see part of the house on Rocky Ridge, but they couldn't see where the van was parked. They went up to the attic, and looked out one of the little dormer windows in the back.

"I can see it," Rachel said, with excitement.

Sara squeezed in next to Rachel, and looked out of the window. She could see the roof of the van through the trees, and even the back door of the house.

"I'm going to stay here, and watch," Rachel announced.

"I'll get us some coffee," Sara said. "It could be a long day."

"You don't have to stay up here. I'll let you know as soon as anything happens."

"I'll keep you company for a while, and then we can take turns. It's going to get pretty hot up here later today, you're going to need to take a break."

"Hopefully, we won't have to wait that long."

"Rachel, what if he doesn't leave?"

"I'm going to get in there by tonight, whether he leaves or not. I can't wait any longer than that."

Sara left to make the coffee, and Rachel stared out of the window. What *will* I do if he doesn't leave, she thought. Just walk into the house, and say "My daughter is missing, and I think she's here. Mind if I look around a little?" Rachel knew she was getting a little punchy. She hadn't slept in over 24 hours, and it didn't look like she was going to get to sleep any time soon. Actually, even if she could sleep, she was afraid to. She was afraid of having that same dream about her mother again. Afraid that her mother would tell her it was already too late.

Sara came back with the coffee, and stayed with Rachel until she heard her sons get up. She went down to fix them breakfast, and was relieved when they asked if they could spend the day at a friend's house. They wanted to walk there, but Sara insisted on driving them. She also told them to call her when they were ready to come home, and she would pick them up.

"Mom, it's only a 15 minute walk," Taran complained. "I'll feel like a baby if you have to come and get us."

"Taran, I know you're not a baby, but don't argue with me okay? I may be acting paranoid, but I think under the circumstances, you would understand."

Taran saw the look of concern on his mother's face, and he did understand. Everyone was worried about Amanda, and if she was all right, and he didn't want to add to that. He felt ashamed that he had argued with her.

"I'm sorry Mom," he said, as he unexpectedly put his arms around her. "I'll call you when we're ready to come home."

It had been so long since Taran had done anything like that, that the gesture filled Sara with emotion. Her eyes stung, as she tried to hold back the tears. How was Rachel coping with this? If one of her sons were missing, she wouldn't even be able to function.

Rachel and Sara spent the rest of the day in the attic. It did start to get warm up there, so Sara brought up a couple of fans, to try to cool it off. The fans only seemed to make it worse, until Sara used a trick her mother had used when she was a little girl. She brought big bowls of ice cubes up, and put them behind the fans. The fans took the cool air from the melting ice, and blew it directly on them. Rachel looked at her curiously.

"Poor man's air conditioning," Sara explained.

Sara tried to convince Rachel to take a break, and try to get some sleep, but the only time Rachel would leave the window was to use the bathroom.

When Sara heard Scott drive in, she went down to meet him.

"What do you mean, she's in the attic?" he asked.

"Don't ask me to give you a rational explanation. She just needs to be there right now."

"Sara, I know she's going through a rough time, believe me I understand that. But don't you think it's the least bit strange that she's sitting up in our attic, instead of being home with her husband, and son?"

"Scott, just let it go okay? And do me favor, take the boys out for pizza, and a movie tonight. I'm trying to help Rachel through this, and it would be better if we were alone."

"Do you mean you're trying to talk her out of there, like she's flipped out or something? I'd better call Michael."

"No, she hasn't flipped out, and Michael knows that she's here. Scott please! By the time you get back, I'm sure she will have gone home."

Scott looked at his wife, and saw the desperation in her face. He didn't want to leave, but she kept insisting it would be the best thing to do, until he finally agreed.

"The boys are at Jonathan's," she said. "I'll call, and tell them that you're going to pick them up."

After Scott had showered, changed his clothes, and left to pick up the boys, Sara went back to the attic. She told Rachel that her family would be gone for a few hours.

"That should be enough time," Rachel said "I saw him Sara. I saw him come out of the house, and he was alone. Look the van is backing out of the driveway now."

Chapter 43

After they watched the van leave, Rachel and Sara sat silently staring out of the window. What they had been waiting for all day, had just happened, and they both sat there unable to move. Sara knew what they had to do, but was afraid. Rachel was afraid too, but she was not afraid of going into the house. She was afraid of what she might find, or not find, when she did. She had put all of her hopes of finding her daughter on the fact that she was in that house. If she wasn't there, she knew that she would have to face the fact that she would probably never see her again.

"We have to go now," she finally said. "He might come back any minute."

"Do you have any ideas on how we are going to get inside?" Sara asked.

"No, but I'll break down the door if I have to. I just hope the dogs are still in their pens, and not loose inside the house."

"Why don't we check that out first," Sara suggested.

The two women went outside, and made their way to the fence separating the two houses. The ladder they had used before, was still lying on the ground. While they were putting it up against the fence, the dogs started barking.

"It sounds like they're still outside." Sara said.

"Wait a minute," Rachel said, as she climbed the ladder, and looked over the fence. Satisfied, she joined Sara at the bottom.

"I just wanted to make sure that they were all there. I only saw three that night, and there are three of them in the pens now. I just hope that's all there is."

"Let's get some tools out of the shed," Sara suggested.

The women went to the shed, and found a hammer, some screwdrivers, and a crowbar. They put them into a knapsack they found with the camping equipment.

Rachel also found a small ax with the camping equipment, and she put it into the bag.

"What are you going to do with that?" Sara asked, with alarm.

"I told you, I'll break the door down if I have to." Rachel replied.

When they left the shed, Sara started walking towards her house, planning to walk around, and approach the house from the street.

"Let's go this way, over the fence," Rachel said. "There's less chance that someone will see us, and it will be faster."

"How are we going to get over it?" Sara asked.

"We'll climb over the top, hang down the other side, and drop to the ground. It's not that far."

It was a stockade fence that was only eight feet high, but the top of it was old and splintery, with points four inches apart.

"Here take these," Sara said, as she handed Rachel a pair of work gloves she had thrown into the bag.

"You were thinking ahead," Rachel commended her.

"Actually, I was thinking of fingerprints," Sara said sheepishly.

Rachel put on the gloves, and pushed herself over the top of the fence. The dogs had started barking, and above the racket they were making, Sara heard a loud groan from Rachel as she dropped to other side. Sara scrambled up the ladder, looked over the top, and saw Rachel on the ground below.

"Are you all right?" she asked.

"I think so," Rachel answered, as she got up slowly. "I landed harder than I thought I would. I'll help you down, when you get over the top."

Sara threw the bag to ground next to Rachel, and climbed over the top of the fence. If Rachel made it without breaking something, I guess I can too, she thought.

The dogs' pens were about six feet away from where they were standing, and they were barking furiously now.

"We'd better hurry," Rachel said, as she saw the dogs trying to bite their way through the wire mesh of their pens. They went directly to the back door, and tried the handle. Although they didn't really expect it to open, they were still disappointed when it didn't. The door was old and warped, and rattled back and forth, when Rachel pulled and pushed on it. She took the crowbar out of the bag, put it in the space between the door, and the casing around it, and moved it back and forth. Pieces of the wood began to splinter away near the lock. Rachel worked at it for a few minutes until the wood on the door casing that held the metal plate came flying off, and the door swung open. As soon as the women entered the house, the dogs stopped barking, as if their job to warn of intruders was finished.

When they walked through the door, Rachel squinted her eyes. The heavy curtains that were covering the windows blocked out most of the light, and it was hard to see clearly.

"We didn't bring a flashlight did we?" she asked.

"I didn't even think of it," Sara admitted. "It won't be dark for hours."

"Something tells me it's always dark in here," Rachel said, as her eyes started to adjust to the darkness.

As she looked around the room, she realized it was the kitchen. It was clean, but dingy. The wallpaper was peeling in several places. The appliances were dented, and at least forty years old. There were a few dishes in the sink, one plate, one fork, and one glass.

"He must live here alone," Rachel said, pointing to the sink.

They moved through the kitchen into the sparsely furnished living room. There was a little more light in there, because the drapes on the picture window were partially open. There was a strange medicinal smell in this room that completely dominated the musty odor they had noticed in the kitchen. They searched every part of the room, looking for a sign of Amanda, but found nothing.

They found the stairs leading to the second floor, and started up them. The smell in the living room was even stronger on the stairs. At the top of the stairs, the first room they went into was a bathroom, with a tub but no shower.

"I didn't think anyone took just baths anymore," Sara said.

"From the looks of this place, I don't think anything has been changed in here for decades." Rachel replied.

They left the bathroom, and went into the room across the hall. There was a double bed, two dressers, and a braided rug on the floor. Everything was covered with a thick layer of dust. Rachel opened the closet, and found two men's suits, a few shirts, and several women's dresses.

"This is getting really weird, Rachel. You can tell no one has used this room for years, but there are still clothes in the closet."

"I've been telling you for months that there's something strange about this place."

They moved into the last room, and were even more surprised. It was about half the size of the other bedroom, with room for only one dresser, a twin bed, and a chair by the window.

"Why would he be using this tiny room, instead of the other one?" Sara wondered out loud.

There was a man's work shirt, and work pants on the floor next to the bed. Rachel picked up the shirt, and looked at the patch on the arm.

"He's a security guard," she said with surprise.

"That's comforting," Sara said, sarcastically, as she noticed something on the chair, by the window. She walked over to see what it was.

When she got to the window, she looked out, and was surprised that she could see her whole back yard through the trees. She picked up the thing she had seen on the chair, with the earpiece still attached. She had seen it advertised on TV so many times, that she immediately knew what it was. She sat down in the chair, and looked out the window. Then she felt the hair on her arms, and the back of her neck, start to rise.

"Rachel," she said, her voice cracking. "You were right about him."

"I know," Rachel said "We'd better hurry, and finish searching this place."

Sara turned, and saw Rachel standing by an open dresser drawer. In one hand she held a half-full bottle of clear liquid. She turned the label towards Sara, and the black letters seemed to jump out at her. CLOROFORM. In her other hand, Rachel held the yellow and red bow she had been wearing the night of their sleep over.

Sara stared at Rachel, feeling the paralyzing fear growing inside of her.

"Let's go Sara, we probably don't have much time," Rachel said as she pulled Sara up from the chair, and out of the room. Sara stumbled down the hall, and knew that if Rachel wasn't pushing her, she probably would have stood there like a zombie. When they got down the stairs to the living room, Sara began to tremble. She sank to the floor, and said, "Just give me a minute, Rachel. I think I'm going to pass out."

Rachel bent over her, and said, "I know how you feel, Sara, but we have to find Amanda before he gets back."

The thought of Amanda, alone in this house with that man, was enough to get Sara moving again. As she pulled herself up, off the floor, she saw the pile of wood in front of the fireplace.

"Rachel, look at that," she said. "That looks like the same kind of wood that we found on the road."

Rachel walked over to the fireplace, and picked up a piece of wood. It was the same kind of wood, and each piece was about the same size. She turned to Sara, with tears in her eyes, and said, "She's here. I know she's here."

"But where can she be? We've searched the whole house."

"We haven't looked in the cellar yet."

"How do we get down there?" Sara asked, looking around the room wildly.

"Maybe there's a door in the kitchen." Rachel said.

The women ran into the kitchen, their panic increasing with every step. They were both now sure that Amanda was here, and afraid that he would be back at any minute to stop them from finding her. They found the door to the cellar, and started down the stairs. They couldn't find a light switch, but Sara had found a flashlight on the stairs about half way down. At the bottom of the stairs, they turned to the left, and searched every corner of that side of the cellar. Rachel saw something shiny sticking out from behind the furnace. She took the flashlight from Sara, directed the beam behind the furnace, and shouted.

"OH MY GOD!"

"What is it?" Sara asked. "What do you see?"

"It's Amanda's bike."

When they began to search the other side of the cellar, the insulated steel door with the shiny dead bolt, instantly caught their attention. It looked so out of place in this house of dented appliances, and rickety furniture. Sara tried to open the door, but it wouldn't budge.

"Why would someone have a drafty, warped door leading to the outside, and an insulated steel door with a dead bolt, in the cellar?" Rachel asked, suspiciously.

Rachel and Sara, looked at each other for no more than a few seconds, and then began pounding on the door.

"AMANDA," Rachel yelled, "AMANDA, ARE YOU IN THERE? CAN YOU HEAR ME?"

They heard a muffled sound from behind the door, and then heard someone banging on the door from the other side. Rachel stopped Sara from banging on the door, and said, "Shhh, listen."

From the other side of the door, muffled but clearly distinguishable, they both heard, "Mommy, please help me. Please get me out of here."

"She's alive," Rachel whispered, the tears now rolling down her face. "She really is here, and she's alive."

"We have to get this door open," Sara said "Where's the crow bar?"

"I left it by the back door."

Sara raced up the stairs, while Rachel continued to yell through the door.

"DON'T WORRY, AMANDA. WE'RE HERE. WE'LL GET YOU OUT OF THERE. DON'T WORRY."

Sara picked up the crow bar, and the knapsack that they had left on the kitchen floor. She was about to go back to the cellar, when she heard a car approaching. She went back to the door, and looked out in time to see a dark blue van pulling around the side of the house. She raced back down to the cellar, quietly closing the door behind her. "He's back," she said, breathlessly, "He's just pulling into the driveway."

"No, he can't," Rachel cried, as she began trying to pry open the solid door. They worked at the door for a few minutes, without success, until they heard him running down the stairs from the second floor.

"We have to hide," Sara said urgently.

This was as close as Rachel had been to Amanda for almost two days, and she didn't want to move away from the door, but she knew that if he caught them there, Amanda wouldn't have a chance. They got as far as the stairs, and heard him running into the kitchen above them. Sara crawled under the stairs, pulling Rachel in after her, as he came rushing down into the cellar. If they had been ten seconds slower, he would have run right into them. They saw him fumbling for the key to unlock the door. Rachel opened the knapsack, and pulled out the ax. Sara looked at her in shock, and whispered, "Rachel, you can't,"

Chapter 44

He sat on the park bench trying to calm himself. He had been here for almost an hour, and he still couldn't get Amanda's words out of his head. She knew who he was. It made him feel defenseless somehow. Even though he knew she couldn't tell anyone, would never be able to tell anyone, it still made him feel exposed, and unsafe. She was so different from the others. She wasn't even afraid of him. He could choke the life out of her with one hand, and she wasn't even afraid. She was smart too, maybe too smart. She had even figured out how he knew the names her mother had called her. He had to get rid of her. Then Brian would be safe, and he would be safe too.

On the way home, he noticed that a few cars that were in front of him, turned down the access road to Eden Pond. It was unusual, because the road was normally never used. He parked the van on the main road, and made his way through the woods parallel to the road. When he came to the edge of the woods, he was shocked to see police cars, fire trucks, and rescue vehicles at the edge of the pond. But, he was relieved to see that they were gathered at the shallow end of the pond, nowhere near the place where he had disposed of his mistakes. He saw a diver break the surface of the water, and knew that they were looking for someone. Someone must have fallen in, he thought. He made his way back to the van, making sure to stay off the road, and stay hidden in the trees. As he drove the rest of the way home, he thought, It looks like I may have to find another place for Amanda.

When he got back to his house, his dogs started barking, so he stopped to give them some water before going inside. As he mounted the steps to the back door, he stopped, and stared in disbelief at the ruined door. He walked into the house slowly, trying to make sense of what he had seen. He knew it wasn't Amanda. If she had somehow been able to accomplish the impossible, and escape from the room in the cellar, she wouldn't have had to break the back door to get out. She could have just unlocked it from the inside. Someone had broken in, but why? The thought that anyone would be looking here for Amanda, never occurred to him.

He walked slowly through the first floor, expecting to see someone standing there whenever he turned a corner, but he found no one. He took a piece of firewood from in front of the fireplace, and climbed the stairs to the second floor. As soon as he reached the top, he noticed the door to his parents' bedroom standing open. He hadn't been in that room in years, and he always kept the door closed. When he looked into the room, he saw the footprints in the thick dust on the floor, leading to the closet door. Someone has been in here, he thought, and they're probably still here. The fear he had originally felt when he had found the broken door, was now replaced by rage. Blind rage at the invasion of his home. He raced to closet, and flung the door open, ready to bludgeon to death the intruder he found inside. But, the closet was empty.

Confused he went to his own bedroom, and stood in the doorway. This room, at first, looked undisturbed. Then he noticed the open dresser drawer, and the bottle of chloroform on top of the dresser. He walked over to the drawer, and looked inside. He searched frantically through the drawer, looking for the hair bow, but it was gone. Who would have taken it, and why? Amanda's mother! Did she somehow know Amanda was here? Did she come looking for her? I knew that woman would be trouble, I knew it! he thought, How could I have so stupid?

He raced down the stairs, through the first floor, and down to the cellar. He was amazed that the door to the room was still locked. He fumbled for the key, unlocked the door, and pulled it open. Relief washed over him as he saw Amanda sitting on the mattress, just as he had left her.

"*She didn't find you,*" he began to laugh, hysterically. "*She broke in, and searched everywhere, and she didn't even know that you were right here all the time.*"

He saw Amanda's eyes widened in fear, and said, "*Finally, I can finally see the fear on your face, and it's better than I ever imagined.*"

He relished the fear he saw on her face, but then he slowly realized that she wasn't really looking at him. She was looking behind him. He started to turn around, when he felt a pain explode in his head. Then the room turned a brilliant white, and he felt nothing at all.

Chapter 45

Rachel had looked down at the ax in her hand. She had thought of slamming the ax into the back of his head, and seeing it split open, like a ripe watermelon. She had been surprised to realize that she could really do it. That she had actually wanted to do it. Then she had thought about Amanda. About her having to see something like that. She had put the ax back, and took out the hammer instead. He had opened the door, and was inside the room. Rachel had heard him laughing, a wild, crazy kind of laugh. She had scrambled out from under the stairs, and run into the room, holding the hammer high over her head. She had seen the wide-eyed fear on Amanda's face, and then saw him turning to face her. Without even thinking about it, she had swung the hammer as hard as she could. The hammer had struck him squarely in the middle of his forehead. He had staggered foreword, and then crumpled into a heap at Rachel's feet.

Rachel rushed over, and knelt by her daughter.

"Amanda, are you all right," she asked. "Did he hurt you?"

Amanda just stared at her, as if she didn't even know who she was. Sara had come into the room right behind Rachel, and now stood near the doorway, watching her with Amanda. She looked over at the man on the floor, and jumped when she heard a groan escape his lips.

"RACHEL," she yelled "WE HAVE TO GET OUT OF HERE."

Rachel looked over her shoulder, and saw him starting to move. She scooped Amanda up in her arms, and ran towards the door. Sara pushed Rachel through the doorway, followed her through, and slammed the door shut. It was then that she saw the key sticking out of the keyhole, and turned it, locking the door.

Rachel, Sara, and their families were gathered at Rachel's house. Scott was telling Sara how foolish they had been to go into the house alone.

"You could have both been killed," he said.

"I know it was stupid, Scott, but we had to do it," Sara said. "No one would have believed us if we told them, including you."

"But you wouldn't have done Amanda, or anyone, any good if he had killed you."

Sara took Scott by the arm, and led him into the living room. Amanda, Brian, Taran and Joey were sitting around the TV. Taran had his arm around Amanda, and she had her head on his shoulder, as they watched Brian and Joey playing a video game.

"Don't even try to tell me that what we did was wrong," Sara said quietly, with tears in her eyes. "Amanda is home, safe and sound, and that's all that really matters."

Michael and Rachel were in the kitchen, talking to the police. After Sara had called them, they had gone to the house on Rocky Ridge, and found him still locked in the room in the cellar. He had a severe concussion, but would live. Rachel wasn't sure if she was glad about that or not. The police were still searching the house. When Sara and Scott came back into the kitchen, a uniformed officer came in, and asked the detective if he could speak to him outside. When the detective came back in the house, he said, "We're pretty sure now, that he's the one who abducted the other children."

"Why?" Michael asked. "Did you find something in the house?"

"There are bloodstains in the cellar, and we're not sure yet how they got there," the detective answered, gravely. "But the worse news is, that when they were searching the pond for your daughter, they found the bodies of four children, two boys and two girls. We don't have a positive ID yet, but we're pretty sure it's the four missing children."

"Oh no," Rachel said, as she sank into the chair.

"Those poor kids," Sara said.

"I can't officially sanction what you women did, it could have turned out much differently, but unofficially I have to admit that we had absolutely no leads on these kids at all. If it weren't for you, who knows how long he would have gotten away with

this, and how many more kids would have died.   I'm
just thankful that you found your daughter in time."

"Thank you detective, so am I," Rachel said.   "I
just hope she can recover from this.   The doctor said
she wasn't harmed physically, but I can't imagine what
all of this has done to her emotionally."

"Kids are a lot tougher than they seem, Mrs.
Palmer," he said, kindly.   "They survive."

Epilogue

It was over, really over. Rachel felt numb and exhilarated at the same time. He was in jail, and would be there for the rest of his life. His lawyer had tried to get him off by claiming insanity. He was crazy all right, but fortunately he was not legally insane. The fact that he had hidden the bodies in Eden Pond proved he knew what he did was wrong. His lawyer brought out all kinds of childhood traumas that his client had suffered. He said that he thought he was protecting other children from suffering the cruelties he had suffered as a child. In his warped mind, he saw all of his victims as cruel children who should be punished. But the jury didn't buy it. He was sentenced to four consecutive life sentences, for the murders, plus twenty years for kidnapping Amanda.

Rachel thought about what that detective had said to her the night they had found Amanda. He said that kids are a lot tougher than we think, and that they survive. That may be true, she thought, but the exceptions can be monstrous.

Amanda had been so traumatized by what had happened to her that it took two months of intensive counseling to even get her to talk about it. She had been so withdrawn and timid that Rachel thought she might never get over it, but eventually she had been able to talk about it with her therapist. Now she was starting to act more like her old self. She was even fighting with her brother again.

Rachel listened to them as they played a video game in the next room. Brian wanted Amanda to give him a turn, and Amanda kept putting him off saying, "Just one more time."

Finally Brian's patience must have worn thin, and he grabbed the controller from his sister. Rachel heard what sounded like a slap, and then heard Brian start to cry. When she rushed into the room, Amanda again had control of the game.

"Amanda, did you just hit your brother?"

"No, he's just crying because he lost his turn."

"Then where did that red mark on his face come from?"

"She did too hit me," Brian said through his tears.

"Amanda go to your room," Rachel said.

"Why?" Amanda asked. "Because he can lie, and you always believe him? You know something Brian, I wish that maniac took you instead. I wish he had kidnapped you, and killed you. I HATE YOU!" she screamed, as she ran to her room, and slammed the door closed. Brian looked up at his mother, with a frightened look on his face, and started to cry again.

Rachel sat in the chair gently rocking Brian, and stroking his head. After all Amanda had been through, Rachel had thought she would go through some kind of miraculous personality change, but now she seemed to be right back to the way she had been. Rachel had also thought that after almost losing Amanda, her own feelings about her daughter would have changed, but she couldn't help the anger she felt.

Brian snuggled closer to his mother, enjoying the soothing sound of her voice. He didn't really understand what had happened to Amanda during the time she had been gone, or what had happened since she had come home. His parents always stopped talking about it whenever he came into the room. He had heard things though, things his parents had said, and things on TV. The man who had taken Amanda away didn't seem so bad to him. From what he had heard, the man only wanted to help children. He had even taken Amanda away because he knew how mean she had been. Brian looked up at his mother, and asked, "Mommy, what did I do to make Amanda hate me so much? Why does she want me to die?"

"Oh Brian, Amanda doesn't really want you to die. Sometimes she says things that she doesn't mean." Rachel tried to explain. "I don't know why she can be so cruel sometimes."

No, that man didn't seem so bad at all, Brian thought. *After all, cruel children should be punished!*

About The Author

Susan Biscoe has been interested in writing ever since she read her first novel by Stephen King. She lives in Westfield, Massachusetts with her husband and two sons. This is her first book.